KAA

08. SEP 94

26 MAY 95

30. JUN 95

KT-233-572

THE DEPUTIES FROM HELL

El Jornado de Muerte, the Mexicans called it. Sixty miles of scorched desert between Paradise and Purgatory. Only one man had ever crossed that stretch of land without water—Joel Landon. And only hate had kept him alive. Hate for the man who had sentenced him to death in the desert. The man who had done this had worn a badge *In Paradise.* Joel Landon lived through hell to put a bullet through that tin badge . . .

THE DEPUTIES
FROM HELL

Chuck Martin

WESTERNS

First published 1964
by Macfadden-Bartell Corporation

This hardback edition 1991
by Chivers Press
by arrangement with
Donald MacCampbell, Inc.

ISBN 0 86220 991 9

Copyright © 1964, by Macfadden-Bartell Corporation
All rights reserved

British Library Cataloguing in Publication Data available

0862 209 919 3454

Printed and bound in Great Britain by
Redwood Press Limited, Melksham, Wiltshire

The Deputies from Hell

I

JOEL LANDON RODE into Paradise from the scorching desert and dismounted at the tie-rail in front of the Oasis Saloon. He squinted at a picture painted on the big front window, and a smile split his dust-caked features. The picture showed a spring flowing from a group of rocks under three palm trees. Landon tied his weary horse and shouldered through the double swinging doors.

"This sure is Paradise," he said to the bartender. "Make mine a big cold beer with a chaser of the same."

The barkeep drew one and slid it down the bar. The thirsty man picked up the glass and drank. A second glass slid within the cupped fingers of his left hand. Landon sighed, drank deeply and returned the glass to the bar.

Landon thought of the graves he had seen in the desert of men who had died of thirst. He shuddered. A deep voice spoke behind him.

"Did you find what you was looking for out yonder?"

Landon turned slowly to face the speaker. A big man was standing behind the look-out's chair near the faro game, chewing an unlighted cigar. A heavy gold chain was draped between the upper pockets of his embroidered waistcoat. A pair of brilliant black eyes stared at Landon without winking.

Joel Landon was six feet and two inches tall, but he felt small in the presence of the gambler. The other man would top him by at least three inches and fifty-odd pounds. Both hands were gripping the lapels of the fancy vest, and Landon could see the bulge that indicated a hide-out gun under the gambler's left arm.

"There's nothing better than a cold drink at a time like this," Landon said quietly and flipped a silver dollar on the bar. "That's what I was looking for, and that's what I found."

"My name is Grant Farnol, stranger," the gambler introduced himself. "Like as not you heard about me when you headed for Paradise from the outside."

Landon cocked his head to one side, his gray eyes drawn

7

at the corners with the squint that comes from looking into far spaces across the shimmering heat waves of the desert.

"Farnol?" he repeated softly, and shook his head. "Can't say that I ever heard of the name," he drawled, "but I'm glad to know you. My name is Joel Landon."

The big man set his lips and tightened his hands until the silk threatened to tear. His black eyes burned with the savage light of wounded vanity. He recovered his composure and smiled coldly as he crossed the room slowly and stood before Landon.

"You're a liar, Landon," he accused quietly. "You've heard of me many's the time!"

Landon leaned back until his wide shoulders touched the bar. His right hand dipped down fast and came up gleaming with burnished gunmetal, worn smooth from constant practice.

"Back off and start again," he said crisply. "I said I never heard of you!"

Farnol stared at the thin tanned face with no trace of fear in his narrowed eyes. His head nodded slightly after a close scrutiny, and he made his apology without loss of dignity.

"I'm unsaying my words, stranger," he murmured. "You never heard of me before, but we should get better acquainted. You have been looking for the last gold mine."

Joel Landon smiled and holstered his six-shooter. The scabbard was tied low on his right leg for a fast draw, and the heavy forty-five disappeared as quickly as it had leaped to his hand. Any gunman of experience could have told something of Landon's ability from the way he wore his hardware.

"Name a man in these parts who hasn't looked for that lost gold mine," he said carelessly. "I bought supplies here in town ten days ago, and I've been out on the desert ever since. I haven't heard that there was any law against it."

"That's right," Farnol agreed and then smiled. "I'll stake you for another look and take half of what you find," he offered. "Set out my private bottle, Zeke," he told the bartender.

The desert man shook his head to refuse the drink. "I never use anything stronger than beer, and I've had enough of that for now," he said pleasantly. "I don't need a grubstake, but thanks just the same."

"Better take it and string along with me," Farnol suggested. "I run things here in Paradise and vicinity, and strangers don't stay long unless they play my way."

His deep voice was smooth and under perfect control, but there was no mistaking the undercurrent of hostility in the gambler's statement. Landon stared into the glittering black eyes and moved back a step. Little ridges of stubborn muscle framed his lean jaws; his hand was poised above his holstered gun.

"That's twice hand-running," he said quietly. "You might be the boss of Paradise, but I don't wear your brand. I'll play my hand to suit myself, and I'm calling yours!"

"Elevate, stranger," a gruff voice interrupted, and a gun muzzle made a dent in Landon's back. "The law speaking from behind a full house!"

Landon dropped his hand away from his gun as he slowly turned. A pockmarked man in his middle thirties was scowling at him from behind a cocked six-shooter. His left hand went up to his faded vest to indicate the sheriff's star he wore.

"I'm Sheriff Joe Bodie," he said importantly. "I'm taking your iron to preserve the peace and quiet of Paradise."

"He's like as not a damn spy sent in here from Purgatory," the barkeep said, and he laid the double-barreled shotgun on the smooth mahogany. "He rode in from the east, and the chances are he met up with those Purgatory outlaws."

Grant Farnol reached out a long arm and flipped Landon's gun from the holster. His face wore the same careless smile as he placed the gun on the bar and spoke softly.

"Maybe old man Tyrone sent you," he suggested. "Him and that pretty granddaughter of his. Gal by the name of Eve Tyrone."

"Never heard of them," Landon answered, and his lips curled with anger. "I drifted in here to do some prospecting, but looks like somebody misnamed this hell-hole."

"You're a stranger all right," the gambler agreed. "This town is sure enough Paradise after a few days out in Hell's Basin. Or didn't you get that far?"

Landon stared at the big gambler. The sheriff had stepped back, but his gun was ready for trouble. The desert man sighed to acknowledge defeat, but the light of battle glowed brightly in his steady gray eyes.

"I reckon I didn't get that far," he muttered. "I didn't find any promising rock, and I came back to town when my grub and water got low."

"A couple of my men have been watching you, Landon," Farnol said quietly. "They reported that you know gold ore and all the formations. They saw you picking away with that

9

little hammer you carry, and iron pyrites didn't fool you any."

"Fool's gold is for fools," Landon answered dryly. "The desert is full of iron pyrites."

Farnol nodded as he studied the desert man from under hooded lids. He held his great bulk erect to tell of powerful muscles and heavy bone. He spoke without raising his deep voice.

"My offer still stands, Landon. I'll grub-stake you, and take half of anything you find."

"Thanks, no," Landon refused. "I never play with loaded dice. It seems that you run things here in Paradise, so I'll just climb my saddle and make tracks for the outside. Good day to you."

He turned toward the front door, but the sheriff blocked his way with the cocked gun.

"What's the word, Boss?" he asked Farnol.

"Landon says he's never been out there in Hell's Basin," the gambler said thoughtfully. "Seems like he ought to see that part of the desert before he leaves us for good. Get him ready, Joe. Talk to him some and see if you can change his mind about throwing in with me."

He turned back to the bar and tilted the private bottle the bartender had placed before him. Landon stared at his broad back and fought down the impulse to leap.

"Walk out in front of me and don't try any tricks," the sheriff ordered.

Joel Landon walked from the saloon without speaking. He had lied when he said he had never heard of Grant Farnol and Paradise, but it would take a better man than the boss of Paradise to cram that lie down his throat.

Bodie herded him down the board sidewalk and into the office of the adobe jail. The sheriff sat on his scarred desk and watched the desert man from under drooping eyelids.

He wasn't the type of peace officer Landon knew on the outside. The lawmen he knew would not take orders from any frontier gambler. Most of them were gun fighters who rode for the law instead of against it. They had a code of fair play nothing could change.

Joe Bodie was different. The deep pockmarks added a furtive expression to his mean face, and his eyes were set too close together for honesty. The price that would buy Bodie would not be high.

"You say you've never heard of Purgatory?" Bodie asked, and he watched Landon's face closely.

"I heard you and the big boss mention it," Landon answered. "What about it?"

"It's a mighty fine place," the sheriff answered with a sneer. "It's a kind of an outlaw town back there in Eden Valley. Like as not the boss figures on sending you back there."

"It should be an improvement on Paradise," Landon answered with a shrug. "What are we waiting for? There don't seem to be anything but skunks in this town."

Bodie raised his arm in a threatening move. Landon jumped him like a cat taking a mouse. His left thumb jammed under the firing pin of the falling hammer, and he jerked the gun from the sheriff's hand.

A boot scraped a belated warning behind him. A vicious blow clubbed down on his head before he could turn to face the attacker. Lights exploded across Landon's brain, and he dropped to the splintered floor like a stunned steer under the hammer.

Grant Farnol stepped back with the heavy gun in his big right hand. His black eyes stared contemptuously at the sheriff who was retrieving his gun from the limp fingers of the unconscious desert man.

"I figured he was dangerous," Farnol growled. "It's a damn good thing for you that I followed you when I did. Ten seconds more would have been too late. Now fetch a bucket of water and slop him down."

Landon stirred when the tepid water splashed on his upturned face. He clawed his way to a sitting position, and his left hand went up to feel his aching head. His scalp was bleeding. Landon stiffened when he heard a derisive chuckle behind him.

Farnol was standing in the doorway with a long-barreled Colt forty-five in his right hand. He was wiping the barrel with a silk handkerchief, but the muzzle swiveled to cover Landon when the desert man turned his body.

"You mentioned skunks," the gambler murmured. "Perhaps you have changed your mind now."

The room was revolving around Landon, and he braced himself with both hands on the floor. His eyes were tightly closed, and he waited until he had regained the ability to balance himself. He shook his head stubbornly.

"I said Paradise was full of skunks, and I'm ready to leave," he said gruffly. "Your kind never takes a chance, so say your piece and get it over with."

"Joe was telling you when you got your hackles up and went on the prod," Farnol reminded. "It's a nice little walk over to Purgatory, but you say you are a total stranger. Tell him again, Joe. Try to make him understand this time."

"It's called *El Jornado de Muerte*," the sheriff explained with a grin. "Mebbe so you can speak Spanish some, the kind the Mexicans talk."

"The Journey of Death," Landon interpreted just above his breath, and he jerked his head up and stared at the gambler. "I get it," he said in a grating whisper. "You put a man out on the desert without water. You set him afoot, and you know damn well it's too far for him to make the drag!"

"That's reading sign, and it isn't murder," Farnol said with a smile. "That is, not legally. We don't want any truck with the outside law, and up to now we haven't had any to speak of."

"They say that lost gold mine will run into millions," Joe Bodie interrupted slyly. "A man wouldn't find it tough if he had a good horse, with plenty of grub and water. He might even enjoy it, in case he was a desert man like yourself.

"Just what I was thinking," Farnol seconded the sheriff. "We could give Landon an outfit, and he could report to you once a week. Like a convict does when he is out on parole. That is, providing Landon changes his mind."

Joel Landon growled deep in his throat and lurched to his feet. His tall frame was lean with saddle-toughened muscle, and his wide shoulders straightened as he stared at the gambler and slowly shook his head.

"Hell or Purgatory, it's all one to me," he said evenly. "A man can't die but one time."

"He can die a thousand deaths out there in that sink," Bodie contradicted with a shudder. "Most of them blow their tops, and I've seen them tear off their clothes and throw them away. Then the sun gets to working, but you mentioned that you was a desert man, so I'm not telling you anything you don't already know."

"That's right," Landon agreed grimly. "And what I said about skunks still goes."

Farnol tightened his jaw and jerked up his massive head. He slipped the gun back into his holster, and nodded at the sheriff as he walked outside.

"Rig him out," he ordered roughly. "He'll get all the walking he wants, and he will find out how many times a man can die."

Landon stepped outside when Bodie prodded him in the ribs with his gun. The desert man's eyes swung up the dusty street and stared at his horse tied in front of the Oasis. Bodie laughed coarsely and reached for a small metal canteen hanging under the boarded porch roof.

"We ain't killers, me and the boss," he said slowly. "Here's some water to wet your whistle out there in Hell's back yard. Better take good care of it because it won't last long when the sun gets to boiling down real good."

Landon took the little canteen and slipped it inside his flannel shirt. He fastened the canvas strap over his left shoulder, and tugged his battered Stetson hat down over his eyes.

"The air is some better out here," he said quietly. "It ought to clear up some more out there in the desert."

"It sure does, Mister," the sheriff agreed with a wolfish grin. "It burns up out there where you're heading, but you might be different. Mebbe you can get along without water like a camel."

"A gent like you wouldn't know," Landon said slowly, but his arm hugged the precious water close to his body. "Have you got it all figured out yet?" he asked the sneering sheriff.

"Just start pointing your boots down the street where you see that strip of white sand swallowing up the road," Bodie ordered. "Yeah; we've got it all figured out down to the last circling buzzard."

Landon stared at the mean face and thought of the last grave he had seen out on the desert. The last one—because he had dug it with his own hands.

Yesterday, just before he had come within sight of Paradise, circling buzzards had attracted his attention. The man he had found had not been dead very long.

Landon shuddered when he thought of what he had seen. The desert sun is not kind to tender skin. He had fashioned a shallow grave in the shifting sand and had piled on rocks to keep the coyotes away. Joe Bodie was watching Landon with a knowing smile.

"One of my men saw you bury the body of that tenderfoot," he remarked carelessly. "We don't go to all that trouble. We figure that's what the buzzards are for."

Landon made no answer. He squared his shoulders and started to walk. He could hear the grit crunching under the big boots of Grant Farnol, and the shuffling stride of the chuckling sheriff. He did not turn his head until he came to the end of the street, and then the hoarse voice of Sheriff Bodie stopped him.

"This is the start of it, Landon," Bodie said. "It ain't much more than sixty miles across *El Jornado de Muerte*. I've even heard there's a short cut, but being a stranger, you wouldn't know about that. On your way, desert man. You won't come back!"

Landon nodded and started to walk. He could hear the two men talking about him and his chances of crossing the blazing strip of blistering desert. The muscles of his back twitched as though he half-expected a bullet. After a time the voices died away, but Joel Landon did not look back.

He had always called himself a desert man, and he had learned many things about the parched wastelands. He walked with a slow effortless stride with his arm touching the canteen under his shirt. He was still walking steadily when the red sun faded at his back to bring the comparative cool of twilight. He told himself that he was one man who would beat the journey of death. A mirthless smile split his peeled lips.

2

THE MYSTERIOUS PURPLE SHADOWS of late twilight were stealing across the desert when Joel Landon stopped walking. He stretched his tall, lean frame at full length in the powdery sand, and rested his head against a towering lava rock. A lizard ran over his scuffed boots and started on some errand of its own.

The advance glow of an early moon was reflected on the distant rimrock of a hazy range of hills. The desert man brought out the little metal canteen from under his shirt and sipped sparingly of the precious water.

His mind went to work on his problem while his muscles found rest. He estimated that he had covered about twenty miles across the torturous sands of the desert sink. Hell's Basin was a good name for the sixty-mile strip that separated Paradise from the outlaw town of Purgatory.

The moon was over the rim an hour later when Landon stretched to his feet and tightened his belt. He filled his mouth with water from the canteen and hung the metal container on his belt. He held the water in his mouth until the membranes had soaked up the moisture. Then he swallowed and started out across the sands with a long swinging stride.

An owl flapped up from a clump of cactus, ghostly white in the silvery moonlight. Landon smiled as he watched its flight. He turned swiftly when the soft scrape of sand sounded behind him. A horseman was coming from the direction of Paradise, and Landon saw the gleam of a rifle when the horse turned and came directly toward him.

"Get those hands high, stranger!" a hoarse voice ordered sharply.

Landon raised both hands and waited for the rider to dismount. The man was as tall as Landon, and there was something vaguely familiar in his bearing. The folds of a blue bandanna neckerchief were pulled up over his mouth, with the brim of a droopy Stetson cuffed low over mean and hostile eyes.

"Hand that water over," the horseman said huskily. "I see the canteen on your belt, so don't try any tricks. I lost my way in this blasted sink, and I need a drink bad!"

Landon's eyes stared at the stranger's saddle, and at a half-gallon canteen of water hanging from the high saddle-horn. He could see the ring of moisture that told him that the canteen was two-thirds full. As he hesitated, the tall stranger jabbed the muzzle of his rifle against Landon's lean belly.

"Hand over that water. Mine is alkalied, and I'm taking yours!"

Landon unhooked the little canteen and held it out in his left hand. The stranger snatched it and stepped his horse back with his rifle at his hip, the hammer notched back for a shot. He unscrewed the top with his left hand, and his eyes mocked Landon when he raised the canteen to his lips and let the water gurgle noisily down his throat.

"Ah," he sighed and threw the canteen to Landon. "That sure tasted swell. I'm glad you kinda nursed it along the way you did. Most fellers would have swigged it up when the sun got too hot."

Landon made no move to catch the empty vessel. It clinked to the sand beyond him, and he was thankful for the instinct that had warned him to drink before starting his walk through the moonlight. The stranger backed his horse, and his voice was a mocking whisper when he taunted the helpless man under his long gun.

15

"She ain't but forty miles across the Basin from here, feller. You ought to do it easy in a night and a day, but mind out you don't fall into any of those lakes you will see tomorrow when the sun really gets to sizzling."

He whirled his horse and started back the way he had come with a burst of derisive laughter trailing over his shoulder. Joel Landon stood motionless until horse and rider had dipped down into a depression. He squared his shoulders and started walking toward the rim of distant hills.

A round white pebble caught his attention. He picked up the smooth stone and placed it under his tongue. An old Indian had taught him that trick. Some of the moisture from his body would trickle to the membranes of his mouth, and it would also serve to keep his tongue from swelling.

Only the crunch of sand under his boots broke the desert stillness while he walked the weary miles until the moon faded in the sky. A chill wind blew in from the north, and Landon found shelter behind a thicket of cactus, buttoning his coat tightly before stretching out in the warm sand.

He was asleep almost instantly, and it seemed to him that he had just closed his eyes when a slanting yellow ray of sunlight awoke him. His muscles were stiff with cold when he sat up, and his right hand dipped down to his holster when a rabbit scurried across the glistening sand. He had forgotten that he was unarmed, and he sighed when his fingers closed on the empty holster.

He came to his feet and faced the east where the sun was rising high against the serrated rimrock that marked the borders of the place called Purgatory. He told himself that he should reach it early in the afternoon if his strength held out.

Landon plodded steadily along for two hours before his mouth became parched. Sweat trickled from every pore in his body, and dried in the hot arid air to leave his shirt rimmed with alkali. A gasp broke from his lips when he stared across the shimmering sands. He closed his eyes and gripped his clenched fists.

"It looks like a lake, but it's only a desert mirage," he muttered thickly. "I've got to keep going toward the hills!"

Hell's Basin was a white-hot furnace when the noonday sun stood straight overhead. The only shelter came from a row of gigantic rocks which stretched away like tombstones in a long forgotten graveyard, with heat devils making shimmering halos for the damned who had died there, thirsting for water and for shade.

No sound broke the ghostly stillness until a crawling shadow slowly moved from one stone to another, scraping through the shifting sand like a snake shedding its skin. A shadow that looked and sounded something like a man who had almost died, and was trying to struggle back from the borderline.

"One more mile," a mumbling voice croaked horsely. "By God, I will make it!"

Joel Landon was on his hands and knees now, crawling like a desert tortoise from stone to stone. Sinking down in each sparse shadow until enough strength returned to his wasted body to carry him to the next. His hands and knees were raw and caked with dried blood. The skin was cracking on his gaunt frame from the infernal heat. But he kept crawling forward, moving ever closer to the hills of Purgatory.

Then a circling dot appeared in the clear blue sky far overhead!

The creeping man raised his head and stared at the great circling bird. He whispered. "I'll cheat you, you damn buzzard! You and all your kind!"

Heat waves shimmered before his eyes as he watched the great circling bird. Landon lowered his head and closed his eyes. His mind went back to the sheriff's office in Paradise.

"*El Jornado de Muerte*," they had called it back there, where Grant Farnol and his henchman had passed sentence. The Journey of Death, because no man had ever crossed that sixty-mile strip of hell on foot, and without water. No man except Joel Landon, who now raised up on his elbows to stare at a darker border of rocks cutting into the desert floor from the north.

A smile twitched his lips and cracked the skin around his mouth. The little wounds did not bleed because there was no moisture in the wasted body of the condemned man. There was water ahead up there in Purgatory, and Landon started crawling forward again.

He had stopped thinking because even that effort required strength he would need for that last long mile through hell. An hour—two hours went slowly into Eternity. The circling dot above was larger now, and drawing closer and closer. Landon did not look up when he paused to rest. He did look at an open stretch of about two hundred yards, where not even a stone broke the blinding whiteness of the sand, to offer a blistering shade.

He was resting in the shadow of the last tombstone. He would stop there until his wasted muscles stopped twitching,

17

and then he would go on to win his race with death. Two hundred yards? Hell! He could *roll* that far!

Now the tip of his blackened tongue was protruding between his cracked lips. He tried to draw it back and almost choked. It was swollen large to fill his mouth with pulpy dryness, but Joel Landon's eyes were bright as he started across the last blazing strip of Hell's Basin.

Crawling like a great snake, with his tattered boots scraping a pair of grooves behind him. Thirty minutes later he was half-way across. Only a hundred yards to go, with the hot wind blowing the scented coolness of dripping water against his cracking skin. A hundred yards of burning hell—with Heaven just in sight.

For a moment he balanced on torn hands and stared at the border of green. His elbows began to bend slowly. Now he was down flat on his chest. He tried to raise himself again and felt his face touching the hot, gritty sand.

A thought flashed feverishly through his mind. One time he had run a hundred yards in ten seconds. It had taken him half an hour to crawl the hundred yards he had just finished. There was another hundred yards ahead . . .

The skin on his cheek split from jaw to cheekbone when he spilled in the sand. Joel Landon lost consciousness. He lay for a long moment without moving. Even the hot air and the shimmering heat waves seemed held for a time in suspension.

The circling dot above broke the stillness with one raucous cry of triumph. It swooped down on powerful pinions to claim its own.

The great bird alighted on Landon's shoulders and folded its ghostly wings. The great curved beak turned sideways above the base of his skull. Steely muscles tensed for the strike.

Brang!

A rifle barked flatly from the green rocks. A swirling fluff of feathers caught the breeze and scattered across the hot white sands. A horrible stench tainted the air where the buzzard had dissolved under a 45-70 slug.

There was silence for a long moment after the echoes from the explosion had died away. A deep-chested Morgan horse broke from the sheltering rocks and came across the sand toward Landon. The big horse fought its head and tried to cut back when the heat burned its feet.

A girl guided the stallion with her right hand and shifted the Winchester rifle from her left hand to the boot under the

18

left fender of her saddle. She swung down and lifted Joel Landon to a sitting position.

She knew well the tortures of *El Jornado de Muerte*. Forty hours in the heat of Hell's Basin would take forty pounds from the frame of a strong man. She knew that none but a very strong man could have made the journey of death to Purgatory where a new life began. She used all her strength to pick up Landon and place him face down across the saddle.

She led the horse across the narrow strip of sand to the cool shade of the great green rocks and lowered Landon to a stubble of hardy browse. His body showed marks of the torture he had endured. His fingernails were broken and raw; his skin was blistered and cracked; his tongue protruded, swollen and black.

"Grant Farnol did this," the girl whispered. "Only this time he picked on a *man!*"

Stripping the blue bandanna from her throat, she soaked the cloth in the cold water below the dripping springs. Then she allowed a drop at a time to trickle on Landon's tongue. She bathed his chest and arms with water.

"He has been sent to us," a deep mellow voice murmured behind the girl. "I have been watching you, Eve. He comes as a portent."

Eve Tyrone turned swiftly and stared at an old man who might have been a prophet from Biblical times. A snowy beard swept low on his chest, and his body had endured desert heat and mountain wind for at least eighty years.

"I didn't hear you come, Gramps," she said in her deep throaty voice. "I found the stranger more than an hour ago. He came across Hell's Basin, and he was crawling on his hands and knees until he went down for the last time. I didn't know just what to do at first, so I hid behind the rocks and watched him for a time."

"That was wise, Eve," the old man agreed. "He might have been sent to spy on us by our enemies."

"Study his face, Gramps," the girl said quickly. "He's a fighter, every inch of him!"

"And he was almost beaten," the old man murmured gravely. "None of us are sufficient unto ourselves. He would not have made it to water, and yet he was so close. There are no accidents in Destiny."

"You can see where I picked him up not more than a hundred yards from the springs," the girl answered with a nod.

"It was the buzzards circling that brought me down here. One of them was perched on his shoulder."

"He was dragging himself," the old man murmured, with a note of respect and an undertone of pity in his mellow voice. "He had less than a hundred yards to go, but he would never have made it alone. You did well, my dear, and I am proud of you again."

"I knew you would approve," the girl whispered, as though she were afraid she would awaken the unconscious man. "He is a horseman from the looks of his boots, and the marks on his clothing. But he had neither horse nor water, and that can mean only one thing."

The old man bent his huge frame and studied the blistered face of Joel Landon.

"He is a desert man, and he has been sent to us," he said slowly, but his deep voice was positive with conviction. "He would have died out there in Hell's Basin if there had been any doubt as to his fitness. He is every inch a man as you say, and we will restore him to health and strength."

"He will be very weak for days," Eve Tyrone said with a doubtful shake of her head. "All the moisture has been evaporated from his tissues."

"He has the look of a man who has lived clean," old Adam Tyrone said, as though assuring himself of his findings. "He will recuperate quickly. And he will have the courage to fight against a temporary weakness."

"I was wondering about the others," the girl answered with a little frown of worry.

"I was thinking of our men also," he admitted honestly, and then he sighed. "Some of them do not think as we do, Eve."

"Especially Shawn O'Hara," the girl took him up quickly. "We were both worrying about what he and his men will do."

"The man baffles me at times," old Adam admitted reluctantly. "Were it not for the common cause that binds us together, I would insist that O'Hara leave Purgatory. His ways are not our ways, but we gave him sanctuary when he was driven from Paradise."

"The stranger is helpless," the girl murmured. "He is a fighter who has used up the last ounce of his strength. Now he must rest awhile until he is strong enough to fight again."

Old Adam Tyrone smiled gently and raised his white head. His big hands were steady when he felt the pulse in Joel Landon's wrist. The old man nodded as though satisfied.

"He is young, and he will get strong to fight the battles

of life again," he said confidently. "Perhaps he will help us fight the battles that are confronting us."

"I feel it so strongly," Eve answered softly. "But we will have to protect him for a time, Gramps. There are those who would destroy him while he is helpless. Men who are as ruthless as that buzzard out yonder was," and she pointed to the drifting feathers on the desert floor. "That one was about to strike."

The old patriarch frowned and continued to stroke his long white beard. Joel Landon did not move, and after a long silence, old Adam nodded slowly.

"It is the coward's way," he murmured. "The big bird would have struck first at the base of the brain. That is excusable in the dumb creatures, but I cannot understand it in a man."

"You could understand if you were that kind of a man," the girl said quietly. "But you have never taken advantage of any one in all your life."

"We will see to it that none of our men take advantage," Adam Tyrone said simply. "I am positive that the stranger has been sent to us, but Time alone will prove if I am right.

3

A CLATTER OF HOOVES rattled out from the narrow pass behind the old man and the girl. A horse slid to a stop, showering sand upon the little group by the springs. Eve Tyrone and the old man turned to face a red-bearded giant who was stepping down from his saddle, and Adam Tyrone frowned when he saw the naked six-shooter in the newcomer's right hand.

"Put up that gun, Shawn O'Hara," he said sternly. "There is nothing here for you to shoot!"

"You're a fool, old Adam," the red-beard growled hoarsely. "Grant Farnol sent that sneaking spy back here."

Tyrone drew himself erect and stepped in front of the unconscious man. His deep voice rang with authority when he waved his hand at the weapon in the bearded man's right fist.

"Put up that gun, Shawn O'Hara. The stranger has been sent to us by one more powerful than Grant Farnol. Eve will

21

nurse him back to health and strength. There will be work that only he can do!"

O'Hara sneered but he holstered his gun and lowered his eyes under the steady and commanding gaze of the old man. He shifted his big boots and muttered in his red beard while his little eyes glared down at the helpless stranger.

"The boys will have something to say about this," he growled angrily. "Glint or Limpy won't like this any to speak of."

"Glint O'Connor and Limpy Bocker are your friends, not mine," the old man answered stiffly. "And while I am alive, you men will do as I say."

His deep voice was low, but stern with authority. A frown of irritation clouded his face briefly when he saw his grand-daughter silently backing up his words. Her hand was on her gun while she waited for Shawn O'Hara to loosen the grip on his own. After which the girl dropped to her knees and held a cup of water to the stranger's parched lips.

A blistered and torn hand reached out shakily and took the cup. Shawn O'Hara leaned forward and blurted hoarsely.

"He's been playing possum, by God; He don't fool me for a minute!"

Once more his right hand made a rapid pass and drew his heavy forty-five. The hammer clicked back under his thumb. He leveled down and covered the helpless stranger, and both shoulders swaggered.

Joel Landon sipped slowly while the girl supported his shoulders against her knee. Her brown eyes were soft with pity as she watched him. He finished the water and slowly nodded to express his thanks.

He looked from face to face, and then he tried to speak. Only a thick mumbling noise came from his lips because of his swollen tongue, but his meaning was plain when he stared steadily at Shawn O'Hara and the gun in the red giant's hand. Eve Tyrone interpreted in a soft clear voice.

"He said that Grant Farnol sentenced him to *El Jornado de Muerte,* the journey of death!"

Shawn O'Hara held the drop with his pistol as he slowly shook his red head. For a moment it seemed that he was going to press trigger, and Eve Tyrone drew her own light gun.

"It's a plant," O'Hara stated positively. "They took him into Hell's Basin with water and a horse. Then they turned back, and he came along on foot for a few miles to make it look good. The man don't live who could cross that strip of

22

burning hell on foot without water. This damn spy ain't fooling me for a single minute. It would save us all a lot of trouble if he never got up again!"

Lying there in the shade of the dripping springs, Joel Landon was regaining some of his lost strength. He raised himself slowly and looked back across the burning desert. Then he turned his head painfully and locked glances with Shawn O'Hara, without fear.

"Mebbe it was a test." He articulated slowly and with extreme difficulty, but now his speech was intelligible. "I was driven out of Paradise for one reason. Because I happened to remark that the people of Purgatory and Eden Valley were not all outlaws and killers."

Shawn O'Hara looked at the girl and lowered the hammer of his six-shooter. The stranger's words brought a gleam of anger to his eyes. He clicked back the hammer under his calloused thumb when he spat a savage question.

"Are you the law?"

Joel Landon started to raise his left hand, and stopped the movement with a tired sigh. Eve Tyrone pushed him back with fingers that pressed three times against the flesh of his shoulders. Adam Tyrone stroked his long white beard as a startled gleam leaped to his eyes and burned brightly while he waited for Landon to speak.

"My name is Joel Landon," the stranger muttered thickly. "I'm a desert man." The simple explanation told why he had lived through the tortures of Hell's Basin.

"You look like one," O'Hara sneered. "You was marked for buzzard bait when Eve took a hand with her rifle. You must have practiced a long time to fool that buzzard!"

"It is impossible to fool a buzzard," Adam Tyrone said quietly. "And that is good enough for Eve and for me."

"It ain't good enough for me," O'Hara growled. "I'd like to know just what Landon has in his mind."

"We are all classed as outlaws back here in Eden Valley," old Adam Tyrone said quietly, and he glanced at the desert man. "What is your interest in us, Joel Landon?"

Landon's gray eyes held steadily on the old man's face, and his voice was clear when he spoke.

"The report is still circulating that there is gold somewhere close to Purgatory," he answered slowly. "I wanted to look for it, but Grant Farnol and his crowd had other plans. One of them included setting me on foot in that cursed sink."

"How long had you been in Paradise?" Tyrone asked.

"I stopped there about two weeks ago to buy supplies," Landon answered readily. "I prospected every day of that time, but I stayed away from town."

Shawn O'Hara leaned forward eagerly. "Did you find anything?" he asked, his little eyes burning with greed.

Landon slowly shook his head. "Every time I started out in the Basin I was watched," he said. "Once I rode within twenty miles of Dripping Springs before I saw the spies of Grant Farnol on my trail. I didn't find what I was looking for."

"Did those men know you had seen them?" O'Hara asked sharply.

Landon smiled. "Perhaps they did," he said quietly. "I led them in a wide circle until they hunted shade. Then I struck out on my own."

"Do you know raw gold when you see it?" O'Hara asked and a sneer curled his lips. "Can you tell one formation from another?"

Landon studied the giant's face. He smiled as he nodded slowly. Eve Tyrone gave him a little more water, and the thirsty man sipped slowly and worked his swollen tongue. He handed the cup back to the girl and spoke quietly to O'Hara.

"I know raw gold when I see it," he said. "Do you?"

"I always knew that some day a man would be sent to us," old Adam said slowly. He studied Joel Landon's face. "Perhaps that man has come," he finished very softly.

"We will take him back with us," Eve Tyrone agreed. "My horse will carry double."

The girl helped Landon to his feet, and she supported him when he staggered the few steps to the big Morgan horse. Her strength surprised Landon. She mounted behind and held him against the swell of her deep bosom. He was grateful for her supporting arms.

"It isn't far," she whispered. "Please be careful what you say to Shawn O'Hara."

The stallion left the clearing at the edge of the desert and entered a curving goose-neck between high, rocky walls. Burned boulders and lava rock from some ancient fire of volcanic origin had been washed down into the narrow pass, and Landon shuddered involuntarily. His escape from the burning heat of Hell's Basin was too close behind him.

"Purgatory," he whispered to the girl. "Is this it?"

"Look just ahead where the pass widens out," the girl answered. "Goose-neck Canyon is about a half mile long, and then it opens into the valley we call Purgatory."

"That other one called Eden," Landon said slowly. "I thought they were both the same."

"Eden Valley is back in the hills," Eve Tyrone explained. "We run our cattle back there, but most of the families live in Purgatory. I think you will like most of them, and I am sure that they will like you. Don't try to talk too much for awhile."

Shawn O'Hara stepped his horse up and rode beside the Morgan stallion. His little eyes glared jealously at the girl's hands holding Landon, and he made no effort to conceal his hatred.

"I don't trust you, Mister," he stated bluntly. "I'm warning you right now that you better talk soft, and step about easy!"

"Thanks," Landon murmured. "I'll remember what you said, O'Hara."

He felt the girl's arms tighten about him in warning. Shawn O'Hara gigged his horse with the spurs and sent him ahead at a dead run. Eve Tyrone sighed behind Landon's broad back, and the weakened man watched the red giant spur up the wide valley toward a group of buildings.

"He has gone to tell the others," she whispered. "Be careful, Joel Landon. If Gramps is right, we will need you very much."

Landon nodded and looked about him with interest. His brain was still numb from the shock of his ordeal, but his recuperative powers were already at work. Most of the discomfort from his swollen tongue had eased.

Purgatory was big; mile after mile of rolling land stretched toward a line of foothills to the north. What seemed to be a village was nestled in the center of the valley. Mud-chinked log houses under big oak trees fronted a public square. The girl guided the stallion to a big community building where a group of men waited on the broad steps.

Adam Tyrone passed the pair and swung down from his fine saddle. The men on the steps were divided into two groups. Tyrone squared his wide shoulders and spoke quietly.

"The Council will meet at once. We have an important matter to discuss, and it might be one that will affect every man in Purgatory. See to it that all are here."

A tall thin man with a decided limp stepped away from one of the groups, the one where Shawn O'Hara stood. The men in the other group eyed him with open suspicion. They were tall and young, and most of them were bearded. Landon

25

relaxed in the saddle and watched in a detached manner while he studied both factions.

He knew that one group of men was lined up with Shawn O'Hara. The other men were watching Adam Tyrone respectfully, and it was evident that they would abide by any decision the wise old man would make.

"We have decided to send the stranger back where he came from," the crippled spokesman began harshly. "Council or no Council!"

Adam Tyrone raised his right hand and his voice at the same time. "The Council will meet, Limpy Bocker," he said sternly. "As Senior Councilman, I am still your Mayor, and I demand a full respect for both my office and for my orders!"

"We don't see it that way," Limpy Bocker shouted, and he hunched his shoulders forward while he stared at the other group of men.

A wide-shouldered man stepped up beside Limpy Bocker. An empty socket watered horribly in his brutal face; the other eye gleamed like a bright star at night. Bocker spoke over his shoulder while he stared at Adam Tyrone.

"What do you say, Glint? Does the stranger stay, or does he go?"

"The stranger either gets out, or he gets killed," Glint O'Connor rasped hoarsely, and his thick fingers caressed the handles of his guns. "We don't aim to be taken out of here!"

"Who would take us out?" Tyrone asked quietly, and he showed no uneasiness as he watched Shawn O'Hara's group.

"The outside law might make a try," O'Hara interrupted. "And when they do, right then you peaceful gents of Purgatory will see something that will curl your hair."

Landon drew a deep breath, and Eve Tyrone knew that he was about to speak. Her arms tightened to stop him, and Landon sighed and closed his cracked lips. Shawn O'Hara was ready to make it a fight with his companions to back him up, and Glint O'Connor needed only a word to send his big hands slapping for his death-laden holsters.

"I said that the Council would meet," Adam Tyrone announced quietly, but his deep voice hummed like a bell.

A hush fell over the group, and then a little man in faded over-alls stepped out from the crowd behind Tyrone. His small hands moved swiftly in the glow of the afternoon sun. Metal flashed brightly to back up the challenge in his slow drawling voice as he addressed O'Hara and his companions.

"You three jiggers step back and talk soft," he murmured,

26

but the heavy guns in his hands were centered on the scowling trio. "We all aim to listen while old Adam makes medicine, and like as not it will be for our own good!"

The little man was entirely without fear, and he was as big as the two guns in his capable hands. His age would be near fifty, and Joel Landon knew that the waspy little man had spent most of those years with the smell of powder-smoke in his flaring nostrils.

"That's Tiny Sutton," the girl whispered in Landon's ear. "He's the only man in Purgatory who is not afraid of those three. Tiny is not afraid of anything."

Shawn O'Hara and his two pards stepped back muttering. Tiny Sutton watched them for a long moment. He waved his hands carelessly, and the two big guns disappeared in the worn holsters on his thin legs. He turned sideways and inclined his head toward the big double doors of the Council building.

"After you, Mayor Tyrone," he said respectfully. "The Council is ready to listen to you."

Shawn O'Hara muttered and shuffled his big rusty boots. Glint O'Connor was glaring at Tiny Sutton, and Limpy Bocker nudged the one-eyed man with his elbow.

"Steady," Bocker whispered. "The time ain't just right, but it will come soon."

"You say something?" Tiny Sutton asked softly. "Or was you just getting the wind off your belly?"

"We said our say," Bocker grunted. "We'll say more when you won't be holding the high hand."

"There's no time like the present," the little gunman answered softly, but his deep voice was edged like a knife. "I might hold high hand, but both of my hands are empty now. Well?"

Limpy Bocker shifted his position and shrugged his shoulders. Tiny Sutton stepped aside when old Adam mounted the steps and opened the big doors. Nine men followed him inside with hats in their hands.

Tiny Sutton waited and stared at Shawn O'Hara's crowd. Six men scowled and came up the steps, removing their battered Stetsons reluctantly. The little gunfighter spoke to Eve Tyrone.

"Escort the stranger inside, Eve. And tell him to do a heap of listening and not much talking."

The girl slid from the saddle first, and Joel Landon dismounted like a man in a dream. His steps were unsteady as he climbed the stairs, and the girl took his elbow and guided him into the big room. Landon was just able to make the climb, and he stopped inside the doors to regain his strength.

Benches lined the walls on each side, with a pulpit-like desk in the center of the room at the far end. Adam Tyrone was seated in a heavy chair behind the desk, stroking his long white beard.

Two chairs were placed in front of the desk. The girl gestured toward one of them and waited until Joel Landon was seated before taking the opposite chair. Adam Tyrone cleared his throat and glanced at the faces of the men seated along the walls. Every eye was watching him; every man waited expectantly.

4

"A STRANGER has come to us," Tyrone began slowly. "He walked across Hell's Basin without food or water." The old Mayor told the story briefly, and without interruption from his listeners.

O'Hara's crowd muttered under their breaths when the patriarch paused. The other men were silent, watching the blistered face of the man who had won against the dreaded Journey of Death.

"The stranger is Joel Landon," Tyrone concluded his talk. "What is your pleasure, you men of Purgatory?"

Shawn O'Hara was on his feet instantly, flanked by Glint O'Connor and Limpy Bocker. His red beard glistened in the afterglow like a mass of fire, and his yellow eyes were savage with hatred.

"He says he's a desert man," O'Hara sneered loudly. "Me and the boys don't believe it, and we aim to send him back where he belongs. If he's a desert man, he won't have any trouble!"

The two men growled softly behind him as they nodded their heads in agreement. The other men stared for a moment, and then turned to watch Adam Tyrone. Tiny Sutton coughed softly and turned to face the trio with his boots spread wide. Both small hands were on his holstered guns.

"I have been here in Purgatory for five years," he began

28

quietly. "Any one who was not a friend of Grant Farnol's was always welcome among us. Farnol sent Landon on the Journey of Death, and he would kill Landon if we sent him back. Landon has proved that he is a man by doing what no one has ever done under the same circumstances. He stays here in the valley!"

The three gunfighters turned their heads and studied the little man who dared to defy them and their weapons. They knew that he did not fear them, and his attitude was one of eloquent menace. Limpy Bocker ignored the threat and stepped away from his two companions. They fanned out on either side facing Sutton, but the little man smiled coldly and focused his attention on Bocker.

"How do we know he ain't in cahoots with Grant Farnol?" Bocker shouted angrily. "There's some of us here who are wanted by the law, and Grant Farnol is all the law there is in Paradise County!"

"How did you know that I wasn't the law?" Sutton asked quietly. "The only difference between me and Landon was that I had a horse. Even with the horse, I just barely made it across that hell-hole down yonder. You three gents did likewise, and you were not sent back. The lot of us would have been targets for Farnol and his crowd, and that bunch is not noted for giving any man a chance."

Adam Tyrone rapped on the desk with a small gavel. His face was stern as he watched the men along the side walls, and then he spoke quietly.

"We will take a vote on the matter under discussion," he said without raising his deep voice. "We have always settled our disputes by secret ballot, and we will do so now. We will abide by a simple majority. Pass the ballot-box, Eve."

Eve Tyrone took a small oak box from the desk and walked across the room where Shawn O'Hara and his men were waiting. Each took a marble from one side, and dropped it through a small round hole in the top of the box. Some of them fumbled clumsily with heads cocked to one side as they searched for the color they wanted.

The white balls would constitute a vote in the affirmative; the black balls would spell a silent NO. When O'Hara's crowd had all voted, Eve crossed to the other group and repeated the procedure. The young cowboys of Purgatory voted swiftly, after which the girl came back to the desk and held the box for old Adam to cast his vote.

Tyrone made no attempt at secrecy when he picked up a

white ball so that all might see his choice. His expression did not change when Limpy Bocker grunted sneeringly. The Mayor sat back and folded his strong brown hands.

"You will count the white balls, Eve," he said quietly. "Subtract the number of black balls, and then we will count the voters."

"There should be sixteen all told," the girl said, after counting the men.

Every man in the room watched as she reached into the box to make her count. Her face clouded for a moment. She selected the white balls and laid them on the desk where all could see. Every voter leaned forward to count with moving lips. Eve closed the lid of the box.

"There are ten white balls," she said softly, but with evident satisfaction.

Shawn O'Hara rumbled in his red beard and moved forward. He stared at the Yes votes on the desk, and then his yellow eyes raised to Tyrone who was stroking his beard.

"I demand a count of the black balls!"

Joel Landon sat up straight when O'Hara shouted his demand. Adam Tyrone shook his head and studied the face of his granddaughter. He faced O'Hara with lips set sternly, and waved the red giant back.

"There could not possibly be more than six black balls in the box," he announced judicially. "The stranger stays here in Purgatory with us."

O'Hara muttered angrily and jerked his head in a signal. Limpy Bocker stepped out from behind O'Hara's broad back with a leveled six-shooter covering Tiny Sutton. Glint O'Connor flanked out on the other side with a gun in each hand. The doughty little gunfighter was caught flat-footed with empty hands hooked above his twin holsters.

"Count the black balls!" O'Hara roared hoarsely. "I don't trust that runty buscadero any more than he trusts us. Count those black balls, and do it so's every one can see!"

Eve Tyrone glanced at her grandfather. Adam Tyrone bowed to the inevitable and nodded his snowy head one time. The girl reached for the ballot box and laid the black balls on the desk one at a time. She counted them in a loud clear voice that ended on a note of stunned surprise.

"Ten!" she tallied.

"That makes the vote a deadlock," Adam Tyrone said slowly. "There has been some sleight-of-hand work in the casting of the votes, but the count stands ten to ten."

"So the stranger goes back into Hell's Basin," Shawn O'Hara said with a coarse laugh. "It takes a majority to win!"

Landon closed his eyes and leaned back in his chair. He knew that the sentence of death was being pronounced upon him.

Tyrone turned his head and studied Landon's blistered face. Then he nodded and set his full lips when he turned to Shawn O'Hara with a little smile crinkling his fine old eyes.

"Just a moment, O'Hara," he said quietly, and he waited until the attention of every man in the big room was focused on him. "Have you voted yet, Eve?" he asked the girl.

The girl's brown eyes began to sparkle as she shook her head vigorously. O'Hara leaned forward, and Landon slowly opened his blood-shot eyes.

"I forgot about myself," Eve Tyrone answered, the suppressed excitement making her husky voice tremble.

She reached into the box with her right hand. She chose a ball, withdrew her hand, and laid a white ball on the table.

"Joel Landon stays," she said, and then her body stiffened. "Don't move, you three!"

Her voice rang sharply on the last words, and the square jaw of O'Hara dropped when he turned to stare at Eve Tyrone. Joel Landon was on his feet with the girl's gun cradled in his big right hand which entirely hid the handle. The muzzle was centered on the red giant's chest.

Eve Tyrone had been standing with her holster almost touching his hand. Her body had hidden the sudden move, and Landon had acted instinctively.

"Pouch your hardware, gents," Landon ordered, and his voice was as steady as the hand that held the gun. "If you don't like me . . . ?" He shrugged carelessly and moved the gun in his hand.

Shawn O'Hara studied his chances. Then he gritted his teeth and slowly holstered his six-shooter. He knew that Landon could not miss at that distance, and his voice burred with anger when he addressed the old Mayor.

"You and her want him," O'Hara accused viciously. "But he won't be here long enough to grow a beard like the rest of us!"

"Leave the lady out of any discussion between you and me," Landon said quietly.

O'Hara jerked his head at his two companions, and both holstered their guns. He addressed himself to Landon.

"Next to old Adam, I'm boss here in Purgatory," he stated.

"We will get you sooner or later, Landon. Are you game to holster your gun and take a chance like a man?"

Joel Landon moved his right hand. The long-barreled six-shooter disappeared in leather, and Landon's voice was a whisper when he answered the challenge.

"After you, Shawn O'Hara!"

O'Hara smiled with his piggish eyes that were deep-set in the red hair that covered his brutal face. He knew the slow reflex action that comes with utter exhaustion, and he had seen the desert man lying unconscious and weak at the Dripping Springs.

His right hand slapped down without warning. A roaring explosion cannoned out before his fingers had touched wood. Dull gun-metal smoked in the gaunt stranger's right hand.

"Your gun and scabbard are on the floor, O'Hara," Tiny Sutton said coldly. "Had it been me behind that smoking gun, I'd have drilled you center, you sneaking son!"

Shawn O'Hara was still reaching for his gun. He stopped the writhing fingers to stare stupidly at the floor. His holster had been cut away from the gun belt around his thick hips, but he had not seen Joel Landon's hand move in that lightning-fast draw. Shawn O'Hara was rated high among fast gun fighters.

"Do I stay?" a husky voice asked softly. "You said something about being straw-boss, next to the Mayor. You all took a vote, and your six men cast ten votes. It's all one to me, but you can take your choice now, Shawn O'Hara."

"What choice?" O'Hara asked hoarsely.

"Bullets or ballots," Landon answered gravely.

"He took both, and he didn't have much luck," Tiny Sutton said contemptuously.

"He can have another try, either way," Landon offered slowly. "But any man who's a loser ought to be a good one."

O'Hara glanced at his two companions. Both nodded with hands well above their holstered guns. Joel Landon watched and waited with the smoking gun in his blistered hand while smouldering flames glowed in his slitted gray eyes. O'Hara stared at the desert man with a new respect in his tawny eyes. It was difficult for him to believe that this gaunt desert man was the stranger he had seen lying weak and helpless behind the green rocks of the Springs. That man had been unable to move, and his tongue had been swollen and protruding. He slowly nodded his massive red head.

32

"It looks like you stay," he muttered. "But God help you if you are working for Grant Farnol!"

"Or any one of us back here," Tiny Sutton amended dryly. "I heard that Farnol was getting ready to strike, and we just might need some help back here."

Adam Tyrone arose and held out his right hand to Landon. He gripped hard and stared at the gun which Landon had shifted to his left hand.

"Welcome to Purgatory, Joel Landon," he said cordially. "If we must fight, I believe in fighting with all our strength, and even after that is gone."

Landon returned the grip with a smile. Every man who had cast a white ball came up and shook his hand. Tiny Sutton was watching the black-ballers, and his voice was sharp when he spoke.

"Take your choice, you coal-passers. I'm backing Landon, and you can have either peace or war. You've all talked big and told it scarey. Well?"

Glint O'Connor took the lead and came forward. "I reckon me and the boys made a mistake," he said, and offered his hand to Landon.

Landon watched O'Hara and Bocker until both men dropped their hands away from their belts. A man didn't usually give his right hand to a gun-passer who had opposed him, but Landon smiled and took O'Connor's extended hand. Tiny Sutton expressed himself.

"I'd shake hands with them three left-handed, if it was me and I just had to shake their hands," he growled.

O'Connor scowled and then shrugged his shoulders. He knew the mettle of Tiny Sutton, and he had seen a demonstration of the stranger's skill.

"We've got to get along now," O'Connor said sullenly. "It means the finish of all of us if Grant Farnol comes back here with an army, and we all know it."

"You never can tell about a war back in rough country," Tiny Sutton told O'Connor. "We'd stand a good chance unless Farnol's army surprised us, which is why we posted guards in the pass."

Eve Tyrone was watching Landon with a new look in her brown eyes. Food and rest would restore his wasted tissues, but now his clothing hung about his gaunt frame like rags on a scarecrow. She saw his eyes close slightly, and she saw Shawn O'Hara watching Landon.

"Grant Farnol wants more than the gold mine back here,"

O'Hara said boldly. "And Farnol gets what he wants. Right now the stranger holds the high hand, but we will be watching him day and night."

"It's going to keep you and your pards right busy watching Gooseneck Pass," Tiny Sutton said bluntly. "And if I had my way about it, somebody would be watching you."

"You've got good eyesight, haven't you?" O'Hara asked.

"Tolerable," the little gunfighter admitted. "Was you asking for any particular reason, or just to hear yourself make talk?"

"Don't crowd me, Sutton," O'Hara warned thickly.

Sutton went into a crouch with both hands poised above his open holsters. His thin lips skinned back to show his teeth tightly clenched. His voice was a low savage growl when he barked his challenge of war.

"I'm crowding you now, you unwashed hulk. Make your pass if you think your luck is any good!"

"That will do, you men of Purgatory," Adam Tyrone interrupted sternly. "We have trouble enough from the outside without engaging in a civil war. It is my order that the regular guards ride out and take their positions. We cannot afford to be divided among ourselves."

"We've been divided ever since O'Hara elected himself as *segundo*," Sutton said harshly.

"He is in charge of his own men," Tyrone explained patiently. "Even you agreed to that arrangement, Tiny Sutton."

"I agreed because I don't trust any of those bush-whackers behind my back," the little man argued hotly. Then he sighed and shrugged his thin shoulders. "You're the boss, Adam."

"Of his Purgatory men," O'Hara added under his breath. "My men don't do any farm work, and we never posed as men of peace. We fight for what we want!"

Tiny Sutton bit down on his teeth and shadowed the gun on his thin right leg. "Either one, or all three of you gun-hung owl-hooters," he challenged grimly. "Now you can either fill your filthy hands, or ride out to do your regular chores. I hate your guts, all three of you!"

Shawn O'Hara relaxed when Glint O'Connor nudged him with an elbow. He turned to look at Landon and the desert man returned the cold stare without winking.

"Let's ride," O'Hara ordered his men. "This is only one day, and most of it is used up!"

He turned abruptly on one heel and stalked from the Council chamber with O'Connor and Bocker right behind him. Tiny Sutton shadowed them to the door with a grim little smile splitting his hard features. He watched until the three men had mounted their horses and had ridden from the public square. Sutton came back to Landon and offered his right hand.

"I'm mighty glad you came to Purgatory, Joel Landon," he said simply. "Grant Farnol outlawed me, too."

"You know him?" Landon asked, and he winced at the steely pressure of the little gunfighter's fingers.

"I know him," Sutton answered shortly. "It looks like you and me will have to stand back-to-back."

"Count on it, Tiny," Landon agreed heartily. "For awhile it looked like I had run out of luck," and he glanced at the black balls on the desk.

"Bullets or ballots," Sutton repeated. "Either way, it will be hard to keep those three honest. Take it easy until you get some strength back, and I'll try to watch for both of us until you do."

5

ADAM TYRONE WATCHED the face of Joel Landon for a long moment, then spoke under his breath to the tall girl. Eve nodded her head. Tyrone came over to Landon and laid a big hand on the desert man's shoulder.

"You will come up to our house and stay for a few days until you have regained some of your strength. We have an extra room and a good bed, and later you can look around and make other arrangements."

Landon smiled to show his gratitude. Now that the crisis was passed he felt weak and shaky. His legs were unsteady when he crossed the long room and walked down the broad steps. Eve Tyrone caught his elbow and steadied him, and she led her horse to follow her grandfather as he walked across the square to a large log house.

A middle-aged woman served supper in the big front room. Landon ate sparingly because of his swollen mouth. He drank glass after glass of cold water, and he was nodding drowsily when Eve touched his arm and introduced him to the housekeeper.

"This is Martha, Mister Landon. She has prepared a tub

35

of water in your room. You will sleep better after a bath. Martha will take your clothes away if you will place them just outside your door. They will be clean and fresh for you tomorrow, and grandfather will see that you get the things you need from the store."

"I don't know how to thank you," Landon murmured. "My skin feels burned to a crisp after that trip across the Strip. I'd just like to lie in water for about a week. I will be all right in a day or two, and I want to do my part of the work while I'm back here. Any kind of work."

"Good night, Joel Landon," Tyrone said with a smile. "We will see you at breakfast, unless you sleep the clock around."

Landon undressed in the large room and placed his clothing in the hall. He smiled when he tried to sit in the round wooden tub, and the alkali rolled from his white skin as he scrubbed his body with the tepid water. A flannel nightshirt was laid out on the bed. Landon donned it and stretched out with a sigh of deepest content.

This was different from last night when he had walked through the shifting sands and had then hollowed holes for his hips when he had lain down to rest. The smile fled from his face when he thought of the masked rider who had taken his last precious water. He knew that he would recognize the man if he ever saw him again. Sleep overtook him before he could concentrate on the hoarse voice of the desert hold-up. It seemed to Landon that he had just closed his eyes when a knock sounded on his door.

"Breakfast is almost ready," Eve Tyrone called cheerily. "You will find your clothing just outside the door, and we will be waiting for you."

Landon stretched carefully and tried to swallow. His mouth was almost normal again. He lifted the large crockery water pitcher and drank thirstily. He wondered if he would ever get enough water. He crossed the room and slowly opened the door. The hall was deserted, and he reached for his clean clothing and dressed quickly. It was good to have clean undergarments again. Landon hummed contentedly and smoothed back his thick brown hair. He stared for a moment into the mirror above the old dresser.

"You look more like forty years old, than just past twenty-six," he told his mirrored image. "You never were much to look at, Joel Landon, but right now you look like something that has been parboiled over a slow cooking fire."

Tyrone and his granddaughter were at the big table when Landon came into the room.

"Do you feel better, Joel?" Tyrone asked.

"I never moved all night," Landon answered gratefully. "I must have slept all of ten hours."

"Take it easy for a few days," Tyrone advised. "The other men can do what work is necessary, but I want you and Tiny Sutton to guard the far end of the pass, down by Dripping Springs. It will do you good to sit in the saddle for a while, and you can see any one who rides across the strip."

Landon nodded. Martha placed a serving of flannel cakes before him, and Eve passed him a pitcher filled with wild sage honey. Thick slices of home-cured ham with fried eggs completed the meal. Eve went to the kitchen and left the two men with their coffee.

"Things always seem different after a good night's sleep," Tyrone remarked slowly.

"Some of them do," Landon answered, and then he shook his head. "I don't believe O'Hara and his pards will be any different today," he said slowly.

"That's why I want you and Tiny to guard the outer entrance to the pass," Tyone said quietly. "It is better to be safe than sorry."

Tiny Sutton rode up to the house leading an extra horse, just as Landon walked out on the broad porch. The little man seemed to know all about Tyrone's new plans, so Landon knew that Sutton had suggested them. The desert man stepped across the saddle and followed Sutton across the square, and the two rode down toward Goose-neck Pass.

All that day they sat in the shade of the green rocks that guarded Dripping Springs. Landon dozed fitfully, and Tiny Sutton allowed him to rest. The little man watched the gleaming strip of white sand from under the brim of his Stetson. The sun was setting when Sutton called.

"We better be heading back, Joel. There's a little cabin near mine," he said, as they rode through the twilight. "You can move in tomorrow, and I'll be glad to have a near neighbor I can trust."

"That goes double, Tiny," Landon answered heartily.

He knew that Tiny Sutton would explain after he had turned the entire matter over in his mind. Landon ate a hearty supper with the Tyrones, and he slept soundly when he went to the big room he had used the previous night. There was a serenity about the big house that calmed a man's nerves.

Landon awoke refreshed and rested before Eve called him for breakfast.

Tiny Sutton was waiting again with the horses when Landon came out on the porch. They rode to the store in the square, and the desert man picked out a new pair of boots and a change of clothing. They rode to the little cabin which was so clean the floors gleamed in the yellow sunlight.

"The women did that while we were away yesterday," Sutton explained with a smile. "Now we better get on down to the springs."

Each morning for a week the two men rode through the pass after breakfast and back again before dark.

One day, Tiny Sutton stretched his arms above his head and studied Landon for a moment. The new overalls did not sag now, and the heavy wool shirt was stretched tight to show the flat powerful muscles.

"It looks like you've gained most of your weight back again, Joel," the little gunman remarked with a smile. "Offhand I'd say that you weighed close to a hundred and ninety pounds. Now me, I don't tip the beam at more than a hundred and twenty-five pounds with my boots and reefer on."

Joel Landon answered the frank smile with one of his own. He studied the seamed and weathered face of Sutton.

Tiny was about five-feet-four. He was past forty, and his slate-colored eyes held a haunted look that always searched the face of every man he met. He was fast with both hands and entirely devoid of fear. He would be loyal to his friends, but Landon knew that the little man could be a deadly killer.

Sutton was staring across the desert floor. His left hand reached for his rifle and brought it closer. Landon spoke softly when he made out the shape of a walking horse.

"Easy, Tiny. That hoss-backer is riding alone."

Sutton growled deep in his throat. "There might be an army hiding out there behind those rows of tombstones," he warned. "You lie back there out of sight and keep me covered while I do the talking, if any. That gent is heading straight for the springs."

Landon slid behind the wet rocks and waited until the rider had crossed the last blazing strip of gleaming sand. The man came on and reigned his horse in at the water-hole. Landon heard the creak of saddle leather when the man swung down to the ground, and then the voice of Tiny Sutton spoke sharply.

"Drink your hoss and state your business," the little gun-

38

man opened the conversation. "Strangers ain't welcome here in Purgatory, like maybe you already know."

Landon heard the stranger grunt with surprise. He leaned forward eagerly when a strangely familiar voice began to speak.

"It was Grant Farnol," the stranger answered bitterly. "He ran me out of Paradise last night. All on account of me wanting to run for sheriff against another man he picked out for the job!"

"You're a liar," Sutton contradicted quietly. "Farnol would have waited until the sun was high, and you wouldn't have had any water or a horse, not to mention that gun tilted out on your leg. Keep those gun-hooks high, Mister Sheriff!"

Landon smiled grimly as he stepped out from behind the rock that had hidden him. The pockmarked stranger stared at him with his jaw sagging. Tiny Sutton watched the two men and slowly lowered his rifle.

"Howdy, Sheriff," Landon greeted softly. "How did you leave Grant Farnol, your boss, back there in Paradise?"

"Joel Landon!" the stranger gasped. "You made it across that dry scrape on foot!"

"I made it," Landon agreed, with a harsh burr in his deep voice. "And you are the man who held me up and took my canteen just to make sure that I wouldn't get across that stretch of hell. I told you then what would happen if I ever cut your sign again!"

"Not me, Landon," the sheriff contradicted hastily. "You say some hold-up took your water away from you?"

"That's what I said," Landon answered. "This gent had a bandanna pulled up over his nose and mouth, but it didn't hide the pockmarks on his face. It didn't hide his voice very much, Bodie. What's your business here in Purgatory?"

"I brought a message for old Adam Tyrone," the stranger answered as he turned to Tiny Sutton. "I'm Sheriff Joe Bodie like you guessed," he added boastfully.

His hand flashed down in the brilliant sunshine while his slow drawling voice continued to talk. Joel Landon saw the move first and flipped his right hand. His gun leaped out and barked to slap Bodie into a turn. Tiny Sutton came out with his own gun, but he held his thumb on the hammer when Landon called hoarsely.

"Hold your shot, Tiny. He's all through!"

Joe Bodie stared at the gun that had flipped from his fingers. His right hand was shattered and bleeding. He moaned and turned to face the smoking gun that had beaten him to the draw.

"You can't beat Grant Farnol!" he snarled viciously. "He's the law up here, and he means to arrest every one of you damned outlaws!"

"You should have killed him, Joel," Sutton muttered venomously. "A gent who would try to sneak like that one ain't noways fitten to live!"

Landon smiled coldly. "I have other plans. Did you notice that the sheriff and me are justabout the same size?"

Tiny Sutton stared for a long moment. Landon was heavier than Joe Bodie, but both were tall, and lean from long days in the saddle.

"Yeah, you're both about of a size," Sutton agreed, and then his eyes lighted up with understanding. "You mean you'd ride back to Paradise in his place?" he whispered incredulously.

Landon nodded. "Who would know the difference in the dark?" he asked. "And don't forget that I know my way about Paradise."

He turned when hooves rattled furiously through the pass. Shawn O'Hara and Limpy Bocker rode up fast and stared at the wounded man. Joe Bodie shrank back and tried to turn his face away, but some magnetic power held his eyes to the bearded face of O'Hara.

Without warning of any kind, O'Hara and Bocker slapped for their holsters and fired at the same time. Joe Bodie crumpled to the ground with a pair of bullets through his treacherous heart.

Tiny Sutton flipped both hands and came out with the hammers of his guns notched back, and anger glinting from his slitted eyes. Landon stepped in front of him with his gun covering the pair of killers.

"Talk fast, you two!" His voice was a gruff command. "You killed a wounded man without giving him a chance for his taw. He was our prisoner. You were put back there to guard the other end of the pass."

"That sneaking jigger was the sheriff of Paradise," Shawn O'Hara muttered without the slightest sign of regret. "And before Grant Farnol put him in that job, Bodie was a wide-loopin' rustler!"

Tiny Sutton stepped around Landon, walking stiff-legged like a dog on the fight. His thin face was grim with determination when he sneered at big Shawn O'Hara.

40

"He was an old pard of yours, eh? And you was afraid that he'd unhinge his loose jaw and do some talking that might put you in a tight!"

"Lay your hackles, Sutton," O'Hara said with a smile. "We did what we thought was the right thing to do under the circumstances."

"You're wanted as bad as the rest of us," Limpy Bocker sneered. "Our bunch vowed to kill the law if they ever came riding back here to get us!"

"Your bunch," Sutton lipped, and he crouched over his guns with his eyes almost closed. "Take a chance with me, you killin' son of sin!"

Landon tightened his jaw and watched the faces of the three men. Limpy Bocker shrugged and holstered his smoke-grimed weapon. Shawn O'Hara growled deep in his barrel chest and refused to give ground. Tiny Sutton stood above the dead man, watching O'Hara's trigger-finger tightening slowly.

"Let it pass for now, Shawn," Bocker whispered softly, so as not to unleash straining muscles. "We've finished our snake-killing for one day. Like you said one time not long since, there's a lot of days that we haven't used up."

"That runty gun-slammer," the red giant muttered angrily. "We both might eat lead, but I'd get him through the brisket!"

"And he'd get you through the heart," Bocker warned. "I'm telling you to call it a draw!"

O'Hara growled and slowly holstered his heavy forty-five six-shooter. His tawny eyes glared savagely at Tiny Sutton, and the little man lowered his hands and with his eyes dared the red giant to take a chance, starting with an even break, no quarter asked or given.

"We didn't do but part of this job," O'Hara blustered to change the subject, and now he stared at Landon. "He had a gun in his hand when me and Limpy came to help, and we figured that Landon had missed his shot."

"You didn't figure anything of the kind," Landon contradicted flatly. "You and Bocker smelled blood like wolves, and you jumped Bodie like a pair of the same!"

"Mebbe you didn't hear me good when I told you that I was high man back here, next to old Adam," O'Hara said thickly. "That means you take your orders from me. I'll do the thinking for those who pack six-shooters!"

"Since when?" Tiny Sutton asked in a thin whisper. "I've never been without my hardware, and up to now you never

41

passed me an order. If you're starting to do same right now, you better get ready to back them up with smoke!"

"I was talking to Landon," O'Hara grunted, and he refused to meet Sutton's baleful glance.

"I heard you the first time," the desert man said carelessly, and then his voice changed. "Now you two killers get busy and bury your dead!"

O'Hara sucked in a startled breath and turned toward his horse. Sutton was after him like a cat, with the muzzle of his gun boring into the broad muscular back.

"The shovels are behind those rocks," Sutton purred. He reached down and emptied the tied-down holsters on O'Hara's powerful legs.

Shawn O'Hara whirled his big bulk and roared like an infuriated bull. He stopped abruptly when he saw Landon unbuckle his heavy gunbelt and place it carefully on a smooth flat rock. His little eyes flamed with a savage light when Landon faced him with empty hands.

"You might shoot me in the back some dark night, Shawn O'Hara," Landon said quietly. "I don't like you any better than you like me. Perhaps you and I had better decide who is second to old Adam Tyrone back here in Purgatory!"

O'Hara knotted his big fists and leaned forward eagerly. Limpy Bocker stood back with a startled gleam in his hooded eyes. Tiny Sutton stared for a moment, and then he barked angrily.

"Use a gun, Joel. That big ape is the dirtiest skull-and-knuckle fighter who ever rode across Hell's Basin!"

"Afraid, eh?" O'Hara sneered, and he turned his back on Sutton. "You keep out of it, runt. Your pard made the offer, and I don't mean to shovel any dirt."

"You'll shovel dirt," Landon said coldly. "You meant to kill me the day I crawled across that last mile. I was down with my head under me, and you had your gun in your hand, and it ready to go. This is one time I mean to keep you honest. How do you want it?"

"Teeth, boots, and maulies," the red giant answered without hesitation. "No holts barred, and when I get through with you, you'll wish you were in Bodie's place !"

"Take it to him, Shawn," Limpy Bocker urged hoarsely. "Before he turns yellow and changes his mind!"

"I changed my mind the day I got here," Landon said slowly. "When I looked up and saw O'Hara getting ready to hunt

42

some glory, and me helpless. Bring it to me, O'Hara," he said in a low whisper.

6

SHAWN O'HARA LEAPED at Landon with both arms pumping like flails and battered him back. O'Hara followed him with a grin of triumph spreading over his bearded face. Landon stopped his backward flight and jabbed twice with his left fist. O'Hara blinked when knuckles dimmed his sight. A hard right swept against his chin, and a blow knocked his head into position for the piledriver that followed through and jarred every tooth in his clenched jaws.

His forward advance was stopped instantly. He shivered like a tall pine that has been struck by lightning, his knees buckled and O'Hara pitched to the ground.

"Joel Landon! I thought you were different, and now I find you..." Eve Landon's voice broke off abruptly when she saw the body of the Paradise sheriff on the ground. Her lips parted in a gasp of horror. Sutton made a swift move and covered Limpy Bocker with his right-hand gun. His voice was low and casual when he spoke to the girl.

"Those two drew on him without warning, Eve, and they killed him the same way. Joel and me figured it was only decent for them to bury him and we still think the same way."

Eve went to Landon and touched his arm.

"You know what that means now?"

"It means that Farnol can come in here legally now," he answered.

"There will be more killings," Bocker said hoarsely. "Farnol won't let this pass. He only framed it for an excuse to come back here, and make it look legal."

"You knew that?" Landon asked slowly. "You knew just what Farnol had planned, and then you and O'Hara killed Bodie to further Grant Farnol's scheme?"

"We did it to beat him at his own game," Bocker growled. "Bodie was a rustler and he had a killing coming. When you got chicken-hearted, me and Shawn did your work for you!"

Landon pointed at the shovels. "Now you can do your own work," he said softly. "Start digging!"

43

Bocker glared, and then he reached for a shovel. He was digging when Adam Tyrone rode down the pass on his roan gelding. Tyrone watched Bocker, and O'Hara sat up rubbing his jaw. Then old Adam saw Bodie's body.

"Who killed him?" he asked in a hushed voice.

"Those two wolves did it," Sutton answered grimly. "It was just what Grant Farnol wanted to happen. He owns all of Paradise, and he wants these valleys."

O'Hara took a stand beside Bocker. "Landon was talking some about riding into Paradise disguised as Bodie, boss," he said to Tyrone. "Then he could tell Farnol all about us back here."

Eve Tyrone listened and faced Landon. "I am asking for the return of my gun, Joel Landon," she said stiffly.

Landon drew the weapon and handed it to the girl. Tiny Sutton made a smooth pass with his left hand. He drew his spare weapon and tendered it to Landon by the barrel.

"I'll lend you one of mine, pard," he said quietly. "You need one."

"You want him to be a killer, Tiny Sutton!" the girl accused. "He shot one man today with my gun, and I was acting to prevent him from shooting another!"

"He can shoot the next one with mine," Sutton said evenly. "I figured you to know better, Miss Eve. Both of those curly wolves were waiting to catch Joel empty-handed like they caught Bodie."

Eve Tyrone whirled her horse and rode back up the pass. When the grave was finished, Joe Bodie was placed in it. Adam Tyrone removed his hat, offered a brief prayer, and ordered O'Hara and Bocker to fill the grave. He stepped close to Landon and spoke quietly.

"You are not to leave Purgatory until I give the word, Joel Landon," he said. When Landon stared at him in silence, Tyrone stepped closer and whispered, "We might need you, Eve and me."

"Me and Shawn will be getting back to our posts," O'Hara said to Tyrone. "I'm still rodding my own men."

Sutton and Landon had little to say to each other until they rode back to their cabins. Landon had finished his simple supper when Sutton rode over as darkness covered the valley. Sutton took a seat on the step and spoke with his lips close to Landon's ear.

"They're gone, pard. O'Hara rode out of the pass with

Bocker and O'Connor, and they'll let on they were looking after the cattle."

"Does old Adam know?" Landon asked.

Sutton frowned. "They are fighting men, and they ride where the fighting might be," he answered. "Tyrone has expected the outside law to ride in, and they tried. Two deputy marshals were killed in Paradise, and both were supposed to have been top gun-hands."

"How did old Adam ever come to be outlawed?" Landon asked with a frown.

"Farnol tried to collect taxes from old Adam," Sutton explained. "Farnol was the tax collector right enough, but he raised the appraisals until old Adam couldn't meet the raise. Eve's father killed a deputy sheriff who tried to evict them, and a posse killed Jesse Tyrone from the brush. Jesse was old Adam's only son."

"What about you?" Landon asked quietly.

"I was the sheriff down there in Paradise before Farnol got in power," Sutton said stiffly. "He stuffed the ballot boxes, elected one of his own men, and the first thing that son did was pick an argument with me. He went for his gun, but I beat him to the shot. That outlawed me too, so I rode back here and joined the Purgatory men."

"O'Hara's crowd," Landon said thoughtfully. "When did they come?"

"About a year or so ago," Sutton explained. "Every one of them is on a *Wanted* poster, and Farnol is a bounty-hunter. Old Adam gave them sanctuary, and then you came."

Landon did not answer for a time. Then he repeated softly: "Then I came."

"Just another prospector," Sutton said. "And you nearly died like those other two I was telling you about."

The two men smoked in the darkness for several moments. Then Landon said quietly: "Those other two were United States Deputy marshals."

"Yeah," the little gunfighter agreed, and he held out his left hand. "Eve asked me to give you this when we were alone. She found it the day you staggered in from Hell's Basin."

Landon stiffened when his fingers touched a bit of smooth metal. He was silent for a time, and then he said quietly, "I wondered what had become of it."

"There's a warrant out against me for murder," Sutton said bitterly. "I can't get out to square the charge. I've been part of the law ever since I was old enough to vote, and now I'm branded an owl-shooter on the dodge!"

Landon leaned forward and stared at Sutton. "You knew I was a lawman before Eve gave you my badge, Tiny."

"I've packed the star long enough to know all the signs," the little man answered. "I could tell from the tone of your voice, and from the hang of your holster even when it was empty."

"Hold up your right hand," Landon said abruptly. "Say your *'I do's'* after me!"

He murmured an oath of allegiance when Sutton raised his right hand. The little gunman repeated the oath from memory. There was a humming note of satisfaction in Landon's deep voice as he gripped Sutton's hand.

"That makes you a special deputy marshal. Marshal Bronson remembered you. He told me to deputize you if you were the Tiny Sutton he knew before Grant Farnol took over Paradise."

"Old Adam was right," Sutton said huskily, "when he said a man had been sent to us. I knew you were lawman from hocks to horns, and O'Hara's crowd has the same general idea."

"They don't know for sure," Landon said. "You say they headed for Paradise?"

"Like homing pigeons, and it ain't the first time," Sutton answered sourly. "I can't make out for sure if they are Farnol's men, or meaning to beat him to the grab."

"Can you get a couple of fast horses?" Landon asked.

"I've got them geared and ready to go," Sutton said. "Tied in back of my shack, with water-bags on the saddle-horns. "I reckon you know what will happen if we are seen in Paradise?"

Landon shrugged. "The safest place in time of danger is right in the middle of it," he said lightly. "We will go right to Farnol's house."

One of the young cowboys was guarding the inner pass, and after speaking briefly, Sutton and Landon rode through. They were stopped again by two men armed with rifles at Dripping Springs.

"We're riding for old Adam," Sutton said gruffly. "And we're looking for O'Hara."

"You can see him in the morning," one of the guards said tersely. "He will be looking for you first. Ride on back!"

"Don't move, you two," Landon said sternly, and he covered the pair with his six-shooter. "This is the law speaking. I'm arresting you for robbery and murder. Tie them up, Tiny!"

Both men dropped their rifles. They showed no fear as Sutton tied their hands behind their backs with rawhide thongs.

"We ain't in jail yet," one of them sneered. "O'Hara and Limpy are expecting you to ride out."

"That makes us even," Landon said. "Bring out their horses, Tiny. There is someone waiting for us out yonder."

Stars were lighting the desert when they rode north across the Basin. Three hours later they came to a clump of tamarind trees which hid a little board cabin. Landon whistled softly and waited in the darkness. A shadow broke away from a copse of trees and came directly to Landon.

"It's Smiley," he called guardedly. "Who have you got there, Joel?"

Landon dismounted and shook hands with the stocky stranger. "I knew you'd be here, Smiley," he said quietly. "These men are Federal prisoners. Take them outside before daylight, and tell Marshal Bronson I'm all right."

"I thought you were done for," Smiley said in a whisper. "Who's your pard?"

"Tiny Sutton is now a special deputy," Landon explained. "He used to be sheriff of Paradise."

"Heard plenty about you, Sutton," Smiley said as he shook hands. "I was in Paradise a couple of hours ago. I saw Shawn O'Hara ride in with two other men, and they went to Farnol's house. I listened from that hideaway we arranged before you got in that jam with Farnol. Did they kill Joe Bodie, the sheriff?"

"They did," Landon answered grimly. "Now Farnol can ride back there to Purgatory and do it the law-way."

"Do you want me to ride out for help?" Smiley asked. "We can gag these hombres and leave them in the shack here."

Landon shook his head. "Too many men would arouse suspicion," he answered. "You take the prisoners down to Slag City and get back as soon as you can."

"What about you, Joel?" Smiley asked nervously. "You know what happened to those other men of ours when Farnol found out who they were."

"Don't worry about me," Landon replied. "Tiny and I will slip up to Farnol's place for a look, and we will prob-

47

ably listen some more. You head out with these two, and don't forget that the posters said—'dead or alive.' You know what to do if they kick up a fuss."

He nudged Sutton when the two prisoners twisted uneasily. Smiley walked back to the shed behind the house and led out a long-legged sorrel. He came back, tied the lead reins to his saddle and gripped hands with Landon.

"Take care of yourself, lawman," he muttered. "Don't forget what happened to those pards of ours, if you ever get Grant Farnol under your sights!"

Landon nodded and watched Smiley ride away with the prisoners. He mounted his horse and faced toward the lights of Paradise in the distance. Sutton was curious about the hideaway Smiley had mentioned, but he held his tongue and waited for Landon to explain.

"I reckon you know Farnol's place," Landon broke the silence. "It sets quite a way back from town, and we broke open an entrance under the left side of the house. We can tie our horses back in the trees, but keep your hand close to your gun."

"It's a habit with me," the ex-sheriff answered grimly. "And I seldom throw off my shots."

"Hold your temper in check," Landon warned. "You've been on the dodge for a long time, but we've got to work within the law. Remember that, Tiny."

"I'll remember, Joel," Sutton promised, but his voice held a low rumble of threat. "I'll remember good unless that big curly wolf makes a pass for his gun."

Landon let it go at that. He mended the pace and bore away from the yellow lights of Paradise. Neither spoke again until they came within sight of a long rambling house located in a grove of desert willows. They swung down and tied their horses with slipknots that could be released with a single pull. Landon whispered softly.

"Keep right behind me, and watch where you step. If they get us, those Purgatory men won't have a chance. C'mon!"

7

ONLY THE CHIRPING noises of desert crickets disturbed the stillness, and no lights were visible from the unwashed windows or Farnol's house. Landon dropped to his knees and crawled under a mesquite bush with outthrust branches. A hand touched his boot to tell him that the little gunfighter was hugging his shadow.

Landon gently pushed an old board away and crawled through a dark opening under the house. Tiny Sutton followed blindly, but he paused when he heard voices coming from a spot just ahead. A hand touched his arm and drew him closer. A finger of light spattered the inky darkness when Landon moved a piece of tin with one finger.

"Look," the deputy marshal whispered.

Sutton touched the piece of tin and applied one eye to the small crack. Landon was doing the same thing two feet to the right. The little ex-sheriff caught his breath sharply at what he saw.

Shawn O'Hara was seated facing Farnol at a little table. Limpy Bocker and Glint O'Conner were leaning against the door.

"You say he only wounded Joe Bodie?" the big gambler asked sharply. "You mean Landon didn't kill him?"

"Me and Limpy killed Bodie," O'Hara boasted. "Sutton and Landon would have tried to make him talk."

Farnol's eyes glittered in the yellow lamplight. He chewed on a black cigar and stared at Shawn O'Hara without winking.

"I control all of Paradise, but I want Purgatory and that other valley of Eden. You gents know why without me telling you."

"It's that lost gold mine," Shawn O'Hara interrupted. "It's my guess old Adam Tyrone knows where it's located."

"He won't tell if he does," O'Connor grunted. "You couldn't make that old man tell!"

Farnol turned his head slowly and stared at the one-eyed man. For a time he did not speak. O'Connor twisted uneasily.

"Tyrone will talk," Farnol announced coldly. "When we start burning the bottoms of his feet, he won't hold out long. Fire is one thing that will change a man's mind fast!"

Landon felt the little man at his side begin to squirm. Tiny Sutton was breathing hard, and Landon touched him with a hand. Sutton quivered with anger, but he controlled himself and stared through his peep-hole.

Even Glint O'Connor shuddered when Farnol made his statement with no show of emotion. O'Connor lowered his eyes and changed the subject.

"There's close to three thousand head of cattle back there in Purgatory," he muttered. "They would bring a heap of money on the market right now."

"Cattle," Farnol sneered. "The cattle goes to you fellows for helping me with my plans. I can't get in as long as old Adam Tyrone and his men are organized for war, and you can't get the cattle out. That's the only reason we are working together."

He turned to O'Hara with a sly grin curling his lips. "How's the girl?" he asked quietly.

"Like always," and Shawn O'Hara shrugged his heavy shoulders. "It's my guess she's in love with that damn lawman, only he hasn't found it out yet. Like I told you, it was Eve who dragged him across that last strip of sand after he had passed clean out. We've got to watch him, Farnol!"

Landon was scarcely breathing as he listened and learned that his occupation was known. He thought of the other two deputies who had preceded him. His eyes narrowed in the darkness as he watched the boss of Paradise through the tiny crack.

Farnol clenched one big hand. "I wanted to kill him," he muttered. "But I was afraid it would bring in the outside law before we were ready to make our strike. The Federal law means the whole damn government, and they might ask some embarrassing questions."

O'Hara agreed. "If Landon gets word to the outfit down there at Slag City, we'd have some fighting to do to get out of here alive."

"How Joel Landon lived out there in Hell's Basin is beyond me," Farnol said savagely. "Especially after Joe Bodie rode out and took the water away from him. We started Landon with only a small canteen, and he had most of it left when Bodie rode up behind a rifle with a bandanna over his face, and took the canteen away from him."

"It would have saved all this trouble if Bodie had finished him off that night," O'Hara growled.

"He claims to be a desert man," Limpy Bocker sneered. "His tongue was sticking out of his mouth a foot when Eve Tyrone found him, and there was a big buzzard sitting on his shoulder, getting ready to rip out his brains!"

"Funny," Farnol said musingly. "Most times, the buzzards won't touch a thing that's alive."

"I reckon he fooled the buzzard in more ways than one," O'Connor said. "He sure looked like he was dead from

50

where we were watching. He was face-down in the sand, and he hadn't moved for a considerable time. I'll say this for Eve Tyrone; she's a right good shot with a rifle."

"She could use a six-shooter just as good if she wasn't so set against killing," O'Hara muttered. "Seems like she never did get over that time her Dad was killed."

At mention of the girl's name, Grant Farnols' face changed expressions. His lips moved slowly, and his black eyes gleamed under the yellow light until he lowered the heavy lids to hide the lustful expression that made Landon writhe inwardly. None of the three men seemed to notice, and then O'Hara changed the conversation.

"Him and Tiny Sutton are pards now. Sutton claims he'll get you if it's the last mortal thing he does."

"It would be," Farnol said quietly. "He's the only man I ever missed with a hand gun, and that was only because he was so damn small. I won't miss him next time," he promised grimly.

Landon held his breath when he felt the thin wall begin to tremble against his hands. He knew that Tiny Sutton was filled with a terrible rage and a desire to face the man who had wrecked his life. Landon also knew that Sutton was entirely without fear and would willingly face all four of the unsuspecting men without aid.

He reached out a hand and gripped the little gunfighter in the darkness. Tiny Sutton jerked back like a spring. Then he sighed deeply and relaxed his straining muscles.

Grant Farnol was leaning back in his chair with his eyes half closed. He opened them suddenly and stared at Shawn O'Hara without winking. The red-bearded giant tried to match glances with the gambler and was forced to look away first. Farnol smiled with satisfaction and nodded his head.

"Tomorrow night," he said quietly, "your men will be guarding the pass, and the law of Paradise will ride in and take Purgatory. I have waited long enough. The time has come for positive action. And O'Hara?"

O'Hara turned his head and forced his eyes to meet the big man's gaze. The black eyes seemed to penetrate and look right through him. He wet his thick lips and answered in a hoarse whisper.

"Yeah, boss."

"We don't want any other law back there when we arrive," Farnol said very slowly, and he emphasized each slowly spoken word. "Perhaps you understand what I mean, Shawn."

O'Hara grinned wolfishly and winked at his two companions. O'Connor nodded and returned the wink with his one good eye. Limpy Bocker was rubbing the handle of his gun, and the red giant laughed coarsely.

"We get you, Grant. There will be two new graves down behind Dripping Springs when you ride through with the boys," he promised. "I never did like Tiny Sutton, and I hate the guts of that deputy marshal."

Landon gripped his companion's arm and backed out through the narrow tunnel. The two men crawled under the prickly-pear cactus, and they ran back to the trees where they had left the horses tethered in the deep shadows. Neither spoke until they had mounted and were well away from the rambling old house.

Tiny Sutton took the lead and struck out on a quartering course across the glittering sands of Hells' Basin. There were short-cuts even in the desert, and the little ex-sheriff knew them all. The night air was cool from a northerly wind, and Landon filled his lungs and thought of that other night when he had been on foot.

The desert had always been a symbol of peace to the tall deputy, especially under the spell of night. The star-studded sky was like a crown of jewels, and the ghostly arms of Joshua trees and giant cactus were silhouetted against the skyline.

"You heard what Shawn O'Hara said." Sutton at last broke the long silence. "He's marked me for his own gun, and he don't like you none to speak of. I'm choosing that red-whiskered gent to celebrate my return to the law I've carried most of my grown life."

Landon had been studying the desert landmarks. He could have saved many miles had he known the game trails when he was making his first trip on foot. His voice drawled when he answered Sutton.

"Shawn O'Hara spoke about two new graves there at Dripping Springs. For one time he spoke the truth. Old Adam ought to know about those three riding out to meet Farnol. He ought to know what they intend to do with the cattle."

"All he has to know is that Farnol means to try a raid," Sutton argued. "It all adds up, Joel. We can tell him down there at Dripping Springs after the smoke has cleared away."

He drew his gun and checked the action after putting the hammer on the half-cock. He assured himself that every

52

chamber in the spinning cylinder was loaded, and he smiled his satisfaction when Landon did the same.

"It's like old times to feel a gun in my hand and know it represents the law," he said happily. Then his face hardened. "Farnol said that he was going to deputize all his men so that means he kept the sheriff's job for himself. He can make out any papers to suit himself in case he wants to file reports."

"The only reports Farnol means to file are death notices," Landon grunted.

There was silence while the two horses loped along in the cool night breeze. An occasional burrow owl flapped away when the horses disturbed its nocturnal hunting. Finally Sutton stood up in the stirrups and stared ahead into the darkness.

"Yonder lies that row of tombstone rocks, Joel," he said casually. "That's Dripping Springs right ahead."

"It don't seem like we came far enough," Landon protested. "I figured we were still about two hours from the rocks."

"We quartered in from the east to cut off better than ten miles," Sutton explained. "Careful now, Joel. There might be a guard posted down there by the strip. Angle in slow, and keep well down in the saddle so we won't be sky-lined."

8

THE FALSE DAWN of the high desert ripped the night curtain of darkness aside without warning. The long row of stones stood outlined against the white sand like stark and ghostly sentries. Landon raised his head from behind the rocks of Dripping Springs and spoke very softly.

"Yonder they come, Tiny."

Both men knew that darkness would descend again. It would be a half hour before the real dawn broke through from the east; the false dawn was only the advance guard of a new day.

Tiny Sutton stretched cautiously to his feet, keeping his head down below the level of the protecting rocks. His fingers were flexing rapidly to restore circulation against the morning chill, and then his voice whispered through the still air.

"Don't throw your shots off this time," he warned sternly. "You heard what they said. They mean to kill us both!"

Two right hands dropped swiftly to twitch six-shooters against hang. A gun will jam tight in holster leather during a long ride, and a split second might spell the difference between life and death.

Three horses plodded wearily across the open strip between the tall tombstones and the Dripping Springs. Three men swung down to stretch cramped muscles while the horses lowered their heads and started for the pool. All three men jerked around when one of the horses snorted a warning.

Joel Landon stepped into the clear like a tall and silent ghost. Tiny Sutton came from the other side to divide the attention of the three startled plotters.

"Did you have a good trip to Paradise?" the little man asked quietly.

Bocker set his short leg forward and hunched his slender shoulders. His longer leg was bracing him like a prop, and his mean face was scowling in the half light.

"We was riding against a night attack," he answered sullenly. "All on account of that sneaking sheriff coming back here to Purgatory to pull some kind of a shady trick!"

"It might have been smart if we had waited to find out what kind of a trick," Sutton answered shortly. "Bodie might have told us something about Farnol's plans, because he was the kind that would talk when he got into a tight corner."

"It don't pay to take fool chances," Bocker argued. "We've taken enough as it is."

"This trip of yours," Landon interrupted. "You didn't happen to see Grant Farnol, did you?"

Glint O'Connor was the first of the trio to understand the meaning of the softly spoken words. He shifted up one step and glared horribly with his one good eye.

"Did you?" he countered hoarsely.

Joel Landon waited until all three were looking directly at him. He smiled coldly and nodded his head.

"We saw him," he admitted quietly. "And we heard him give you three killers his orders!"

The three dusty riders jerked up and glanced at each other. Shawn O'Hara moved his big red head in signal and three hands slapped down to worn holster leather in unison.

The desert stillness was dissipated when Tiny Sutton made

a double draw and thumbed both hammers of his guns without touching the triggers. A pair of forty-five slugs battered against Limpy Bocker's chest and tore through his treacherous heart before his gun had cleared leather.

Landon thumbed a shot away at Glint O'Connor and shifted instantly to the right. A tiny blue-black hole appeared in O'Connor's forehead, then Shawn O'Hara cleared leather wtih both huge hands.

Landon caught his bucking gun high in his hand, and he fought for balance when a slug nicked his left side. The side-step had saved his life. Landon's smoking gun came down roaring. The red giant dropped his arms and swayed like a rotten tree in a high wind.

Landon leaned forward to watch the big man try to raise his right arm. Then a blur of shots ripped through the murky gloom. O'Hara was hurled to the ground under the terrific impact of the hammering slugs, just as the desert night dropped swiftly to wipe out the false dawn. Landon shifted his position again and called softly.

"Tiny! Are you all right, pard?"

No answer came back to him, but he could hear the clicks that told him the little gunfighter was jacking the spent shells from one of his old Peacemaker Colts. He could almost feel the thick velvety darkness, but he knew that Tiny Sutton was plucking cartridges from the loops of his gunbelt and thumbing them through the loading gate of his hot six-shooter. Then came a whisper of deep satisfaction.

"I'm all right for the first time in five years," Sutton answered with a lilt in his voice. "And you, Joel?"

"You're a killer, Tiny," the desert man accused sternly. His deep voice carried a note of regret. "I wanted to talk some to Shawn O'Hara before he took the long last trail."

A small strong hand reached out and fastened on his arm. The hand drew him to the right, and then Sutton made his simple explanation.

"I saw one of his slugs get you, and you went right into a spin," the ex-sheriff muttered. "Like I told you once before, I never learned to throw off my shots, once my guns have cleared leather. I'm too damned old to learn now!"

"That slug just scraped one of my ribs," Landon answered harshly. "But I got him high, Tiny. Paralysed his right arm, because there never was a two-gun man who could call his shots with both hands!"

"Can't, eh?" Sutton said thinly. "When the light comes on

again, just take a look at Limpy Bocker. You'll find two slugs through his black heart, and a dobe dollar will cover both of the holes. You say something?"

"We were talking about O'Hara," Landon said brusquely. "I had him in shape to talk, and then you cut loose with both guns and smoked him down!"

Tiny Sutton growled deep in his corded throat. It was a minute before he could find words, and then his voice crackled like a gun.

"Shawn O'Hara is the kind of a snake that is dangerous until he is dead all over."

Landon sighed and reloaded his gun. He could hear the three horses drinking in the catch-basin, and he leaned forward to listen when Sutton whispered with a dry chuckle in his bass voice.

"Looks like Glint O'Connor is dead all over, too," the little gunfighter remarked with quiet satisfaction.

"He is," Landon admitted slowly. "He was the fastest of the three, and I couldn't take any chances with him while the other two were on their feet."

"He couldn't see any better with that third eye you spotted him," Sutton allowed flatly. "There's three good outlaws riding the owl-hoot trail on ghost horses, if you was to ask me."

"Listen!" Landon warned sharply. "There's someone coming down the trail—and riding mighty fast!"

A horse roared down through the pass and slid to a stop at the edge of the water hole. A low voice called excitedly through the thinning darkness.

"Did you get them, Shawn?"

"You're sky-lined, feller," Landon answered curtly. "Reach high with both hands, and step down out of that saddle!"

Saddle leather creaked suddenly to set off the leaping gun in Sutton's right hand. A body came crashing to earth when the frightened horse bolted. Joel Landon swore softly and leaped toward the blot on the ground.

"Hold your iron, Tiny!" he called quickly. "I've got him pinned down!"

Tiny Sutton stopped his thumb just in time. He could hear a short struggle followed by the click of metal when Landon knocked the wounded man's gun aside. Without warning the darkness split apart when the real dawn rolled across the desert floor, with the Vermillion Cliffs gleaming redly in the east.

Landon was on his knees with both big hands holding a struggling man by the arms. Sutton took a look and spoke grimly.

"It's Baldy Sanger, and I only got him through the shoulder. I must have raised my sights on account of the poor light, but it's not too late to correct my mistake!"

The wounded man stopped struggling when he saw the cocked gun centered on him. His head turned to the side, and he jerked violently when he saw the three bodies sprawled ungracefully on the ground, in the early light of the brilliant desert sun.

"By God, you'll pay for this!" he shouted. "Grant Farnol will strip the hide from your bones when he hears what you two killers have done!"

Tiny Sutton handled his six-shooter carelessly. He spat over his shoulder while his slate-colored eyes focused on Sanger.

"Do you figure on telling him, Baldy?" he asked softly, and slowly raised the hammer of the gun under his thumb.

"Hold it, Tiny," Landon said sternly. "There's been enough killing for a time. Pull this Baldy gent back behind the rocks and bed him down. He just might change his mind some."

He turned to the pass when another horse came racing through the goose-neck. He spoke sharply to Sutton.

"Watch that hoss-backer, Tiny. And no more killing!"

Sutton took one look at the oncoming rider. He holstered his gun with a little grunt of contempt.

"It's only Whiskey Telford," he said carelessly. "Mebbe he can stay sober now. Those three were bringing him liquor," and he jerked a thumb at the bodies near the water-hole.

The newcomer was a tall gaunt man with a neatly trimmed beard. His dark eyes were bleary and bloodshot, and his long-fingered hands were trembling when he leaned down from the saddle to stare at the wounded man.

"Did they bring it?" he asked hoarsely. "Like Shawn O'Hara said they would?"

"They brought it to us, but it back-fired on them," Sutton said dryly, and then he stepped forward and tapped Telford on the arm. "Your pard is dead, Doc," he stated coldly. "It looks like you might have to take the cure for good now."

Telford turned his head and raised his bleary eyes to stare at Sutton. The little gunman pointed with his left hand.

Telford gasped and then emptied his saddle with a scream of rage.

"I've got to have it! You can't stop me from getting that whiskey!"

He rushed at Sutton with both hands clawing. Sutton side-stepped and rapped down smartly with the barrel of his gun. Telford folded in the middle and sagged down like a worn rope, and Sutton shrugged.

"I had to do it, Joel," he said apologetically. "He might have taken my own gun and turned it on me. The gent don't live who can take a cutter from my hand!"

"You just stunned him," Landon said. "I'm glad you didn't lean on the gun."

"He was a first-class doctor before the whiskey got him," Sutton said slowly. "He came riding back here two years ago to cure himself, but Shawn O'Hara always kept him supplied with enough liquor to make him want more. We thought for a while that Doc had cured himself, and then he went on a big drunk and stayed that way for a week."

Landon listened, and then walked over to the edge of the pool where the three horses were grazing on the lush grass. O'Hara had straddled a leggy sorrel, and Landon pulled the straps on a pair of bulging saddle-bags behind the cantle. He found a quart bottle, and Sutton watched curiously when Landon broke the seal and pulled the cork with his teeth.

"Keep an eye on Baldy Sanger," he told Sutton. "It would kill Telford to break him off all in a rush. We've got to do it a little at a time. We might need him badly later on."

"I've heard of curing a man that way, by tapering off on his liquor," Sutton said. "Now you take me; I can take a drink, or leave it alone."

"It's like a drug with some men," Landon explained. "That's what Doc was trying to tell us, but he went mad and started fighting his head when he saw O'Hara."

He sat down on his heels beside Telford, and poured a few drops of whiskey between the pallid, parted lips. Telford moved his mouth wryly. He sat up with a jerk when the raw liquor bit his palate. Landon held the bottle and allowed him a generous drink, and he was replacing the cork when Sutton spoke a warning.

"Don't trust him too far, Landon. I've seen him go on the prod before this. He is stronger than a man would think."

Whiskey Telford sank back and turned his head to stare

at Sutton. A slow smile spread across his face, and he smiled as though he had suddenly remembered something.

"You hit me a swipe with your six-shooter, Tiny," he said quietly. "I had it coming, and I'm thankful you didn't crack my skull. Not that it would have mattered," he finished just above his breath.

Landon studied the thin, cultured face. Telford spoke a different language from the rough men of the wastelands. His thin hands were trembling, and he looked up at Landon with a plea in his eyes.

"I'm not a man any more," he said hoarsely. "Will you please tilt the bottle again?"

Landon nodded and measured on the bottle with a finger. He pulled the cork and spoke gently.

"You are a man of honor, Doc. I am going to trust you. You can drink down to the mark."

The trembling man reached out with both hands and raised the bottle to his lips. He watched the line until the liquor showed against Landon's finger through the glass. Telford pushed the bottle away and slowly wiped his bearded lips.

"Thank you, Landon," he said gratefully. "It would have killed me if you had denied my request. I will try to deserve your confidence in me."

Landon replaced the cork, and Sutton spoke in a low whisper. "Yonder comes old Adam and the girl. They saw you give him the whiskey, Joel. You better think up a good one, and do it mighty fast."

Landon raised his head and tightened his lips when he saw Eve Tyrone watching him. Her eyes were wide with disbelief, and Tyrone was frowning while his lips worked behind the long white beard. Landon did not dare lay the bottle down where Telford could reach it. He turned slowly with one hand behind his back just as the two riders dismounted and came silently toward the water-hole. Landon was too stunned for speech, and there seemed to be nothing he could say that would help matters.

Eve Tyrone stood by her horse looking down at the toes of her boots. Old Adam cleared his throat and stared at Landon with righteous anger shining deep in his steady gray eyes. The girl set her teeth and remained silent while her grandfather spoke his mind.

"I expected something different from you, Joel Landon,"

he accused bitterly. "Bringing strong drink to a man who came back here in an effort to get away from the curse!"

"We watched you," Eve added in a hushed voice. "We heard shooting just before the sun came up, and we heard Doctor Telford race past the house. When we rounded the turn, we saw you holding a bottle to his lips!"

Landon brought the hand from behind his back and stared at the bottle. Again he tried to find something to say, and the girl waited expectantly.

"I gave him a drink," Landon admitted lamely. "I'm sorry you two rode down here just now."

"Sorry?" the girl repeated, and then she saw the bodies on the ground. "You did that?" she whispered, in a husky choked voice.

"I did most of it," Tiny Sutton boasted proudly, and without shame. "It just might be well for you to hold back your judgment until you have heard the whole story from the beginning. We all knew it was bound to come, and we saw to it that it came our way."

Adam Tyrone was staring at the lifeless bodies on the ground. His lips worked for a time without making a sound, and then he slowly made the grisly tally.

"Shawn O'Hara, Limpy Bocker, and Glint O'Connor," he murmured sadly, with a catch in his strong voice. He raised his white head and stared at Landon. "All three of them dead, and Baldy Sanger wounded."

"Yeah," Sutton barked spitefully. "And Sanger would be dead, too, only it was too dark for good shooting. He was on his hoss, and I aimed a mite too high when he slapped for his gun, but I can correct that little mistake if that rustler don't give up head and talk with a straight tongue, and do it quick!"

He turned to glare at the prisoner, and then he clutched Landon by an arm. He spoke in a low whisper and jerked his head at the bottle in Landon's hand.

"Sanger has passed out on us, Joel. You better give him a snort of that snake-bite before he bleeds out!"

Telford struggled to his feet. He came forward slowly, and leaned over the wounded man. His hands were steady as he felt for a pulse, and he smiled gently when he straightened up and faced Adam Tyrone.

"Don't blame Landon, Mayor Tyrone," he said, and his voice was low and friendly. "That was the first drink he ever gave me, and in my weakness I needed it to save my sanity.

I am sure that I can stop drinking now—if Joel Landon will help me!"

9

EVE TYRONE STARED at Whiskey Telford and glanced at Landon with scorn mirrored in her eyes. "How can he help you?" she asked in a throaty whisper. "By catering to your weakness?"

"A small drink every few hours," Telford answered. "Only when the craving becomes unendurable. Will you do that much for me, Joel Landon?"

Landon slowly nodded agreement. "I'll do it, Doc. Now we better get Sanger back to Purgatory so's you can patch up his shoulder. And you better have a little drink to steady you before you go."

He ignored Tyrone and the girl when he passed the bottle to Telford. The doctor drank down to mark and returned the bottle to Landon with a tired sigh. Then he went to his knees and made a tourniquet to stop the bleeding of Sanger's injured arm.

"I might need some help," he said to Eve. "Will you go with me to my house?"

"I will come later," the girl said coldly. "But first we are waiting to hear about this needless slaughter!"

Landon walked to O'Hara's horse and replaced the bottle in an open saddle-bag. His voice was harsh when he faced Tyrone and Eve.

"You better call a meeting of the Council, Mayor Tyrone," he suggested. "There's no use in telling the same story twice."

He swayed slightly and Telford grasped his arm. "You are wounded, Landon," he said quietly. "Let me have a look."

Landon shrugged. "It's just a scratch," he muttered. "Something to remember Shawn O'Hara by."

Eve Tyrone dismounted and came to Landon with concern lighting her brown eyes. "I didn't know you were hurt, Joel," she whispered. "Please let me help you to make up for what I said."

The desert man shrugged her hands away and jerked his head toward the shovels. His voice was gruff when he spoke.

61

"The sun will be getting high in another hour. You ride back with the doctor, and send some of our own boys down to help with the graves."

"And to guard the pass," Sutton added. "Baldy there is the last of O'Hara's outlaws. There might be a couple more who threw in with him, but they won't kick up any fuss now."

"Call the Council meeting," Landon said brusquely. "Unless you want to lose Purgatory Valley, and perhaps your own life!"

Eve Tyrone backed away with her head held high. Landon knew that she was deeply hurt, and he avoided her eyes. He helped Telford lift Sanger to the saddle, picked up a shovel, and started digging. Tiny Sutton muttered as the Tyrones rode away.

"They think they have seen killings. Old Adam thought he could settle his trouble with Farnol without using guns. Just wait until the Purgatory boys hear the news. He won't be able to hold those cowboys down, and then we'll get some help."

"We'll need it," Landon agreed, and he leaned on his shovel. "The Tyrones thought I brought that whiskey here for Telford," he said bitterly. "They took it for granted."

"Think a minute, Joel," Sutton answered. "The Tyrones are good church-going folks. They detest all the works of the devil."

"I can overlook old Adam," Landon growled. "But I can't understand Eve."

"She told you she was sorry she misjudged you," Sutton reminded. "They don't make women any finer than Eve Tyrone. She ain't little and spindly, and you never hear her making baby talk like some of the gals I know. She can ride like a man, and she's the kind that will side a pard all the way."

"Let's get on with our digging," Landon muttered. "I don't know much about women."

He grunted and resumed working in the moist loam. Two men rode down through the pass and dismounted. Landon handed his shovel to one and relaxed with a tired sigh.

The two men were youngsters in their late teens, but both were six-footers. "That's right good shooting," one of them remarked. "Now mebbe old Adam will let us do some fighting on our own."

"You yearlings get those graves finished, and never mind

62

old Adam," Sutton said sharply. "Young men for action, and old men for wisdom. You'll get plenty of fighting."

The two cowboys began digging. Landon leaned back in the shade and closed his eyes. The wound in his side began to burn. Sutton was cleaning one of his guns methodically.

"I wonder what Farnol had in his mind when he asked O'Hara about Eve?" Sutton said softly.

"You've been here the longest," Landon snapped. "I wouldn't know."

"Off-hand, I'd say Farnol meant no good by his remarks," Sutton said quietly. "But Eve is a mighty fine girl, and could hold her own among all the men in the county."

"Good luck to her," Landon said tersely.

"I'd wish her all the good luck," Sutton said emphatically. "With Farnol riding back here with an army."

Landon sat up with a flinty look in his eyes. "What about Grant Farnol and Eve?" he asked sharply.

"He brags that he always takes what he wants," Sutton answered with a chill in his deep voice. "He wants Eve Tyrone!"

Landon laughed shortly, but there was no mirth in the sound. It was like a man getting ready to kill a mad dog, or bracing himself to walk into a bar-room brawl.

"You're forgetting old Adam," he said.

"It's you who are forgetting Adam Tyrone," Sutton corrected. "That old he bull is past eighty years old, and you heard what Farnol and his gang had in store for him. The girl would do anything to save Tyrone, and Farnol knows it!"

Landon studied the deepening graves with a glint in his slitted eyes. Sutton knew that he was reviewing the long walk across the burning desert, and what Eve Tyrone had done for him.

"Eve ain't but twenty years old," Sutton continued. "He might manage to fool her with his smooth talk."

"I'd like to meet that big son right here by the tombstones," Landon said harshly.

"He'd give a lot to meet you the same way." Sutton added fuel to the smouldering fire of Landon's anger. "He's fast as chain lightning in a mountain storm, and he ain't afraid of anything that lives!"

Landon realized that Sutton was feeding his wrath. "I forgot myself," he said quietly. "Getting mad won't win any wars."

"Cut the deck a little deeper," Sutton suggested. "I don't follow you."

"We've got to save old Adam," Landon explained. "We can't do it if we lose our heads. And we've got to look after Eve."

"If a feller talked soft and asked her to be careful, she might listen," Sutton suggested carelessly. "Of course if that feller was prideful and thinking only of himself, he might just blunder along as usual."

Landon caught his breath and leaned forward. "What might a feller say?" he asked in a whisper.

"That would be up to him," Sutton answered. "I was thinking about what O'Hara told Farnol. About Eve getting interested in a crane-legged hombre she saved from the buzzards."

"Let's walk the horses a spell," Landon growled. "You're going too fast for me now. Stop clouding the sign and tell it straight out."

"What O'Hara said might be more than half truth," Sutton said judicially. "I've watched the signs, and she likes you more than common. She'd listen if you came out and talked straight yourself."

"I'm a lawman," Landon said with a trace of bitterness. "I've got a job to do, and I'm trying to do it. Call it prideful if you will, and then ease back on your heels and do a bit of thinking. You carried the law-star for a good many years."

"That's right, I did," Sutton agreed with a sigh. "Forget what I said, deputy."

Landon stared out across the desert. He scowled when he saw several buzzards circling overhead. One of the diggers called that the graves were finished. They carried the three outlaws to the graves, wrapped in their saddle-blankets. Lasso ropes were used to lower the bodies, and then the shovels finished the work.

"You boys stay down here on guard," Sutton told the diggers. "Landon and I have business at the Council House."

Landon led out the horses and the two men tightened the cinches. They rode up through the pass, stopped at Landon's cabin and washed in cold water. Then they mounted again and rode toward the village.

It had been a long double ride to Paradise, and both men felt the loss of sleep. Landon was dog-tired when he dismounted in the public square, and climbed the steps to the Council Chamber with Sutton at his side.

Something warned Sutton when his boots scraped the top

step leading to the big room. The little gunfighter stopped instantly when Landon passed through the wide double doors. A deep voice spoke warningly from just inside.

"Keep your hands high, Landon! We want to hear you talk, but our orders were for you to leave your gun here with us!"

Landon turned slowly to face a pair of tall young riders. Both held six-shooters in their steady hands. Eve Tyrone stood just behind them with her gun in hand. Her brown eyes glinted as they had the day he had first seen her at Dripping Springs.

Landon drew a deep breath and regarded the girl through narrowed eyes. There was a mixture of anger and annoyance in his voice when he spoke to her in his slow deep drawl.

"You can't do it this time. I've surrendered my gun for the last time. You know why without me saying!"

Eve Tyrone came forward and breasted up to him until the muzzle of her gun touched his arching chest. Her throaty voice vibrated with determination when she spoke through clenched teeth.

"I am taking your gun, Joel Landon. Or else!"

Landon lowered his right hand slowly and gripped the butt of his borrowed forty-five. There was a steely glint in his gray eyes when his lips moved slowly.

"Shoot," he said, and his voice was low and even. "I don't fight women, but you can't take my gun!"

Tiny Sutton eased through the doors without making a sound until his deep voice warned the slender cowboys.

"You two Purgatory men. Lay those guns of yours on the table, or I'm laying you both on the floor!"

Both boys knew Tiny Sutton and his peculiar abilities. Their guns thudded to the table before the girl could interfere. They stepped back when Sutton came into the room.

Eve Tyrone gasped and jerked her eyes away from the face of Landon. The desert man was staring down at the gun against his heart. His right hand moved swiftly with fingers gripping the gun, his left thumb locked under the hammer.

Eve Tyrone jerked back and tried to wrest the weapon free. Landon stiffened his fingers and stepped away with the gun in his left hand. Then he came forward again and pouched the weapon deep in the empty holster on the girl's right leg.

"You didn't have the hammer eared all the way back,"

he reproved softly. "You might remember that just in case we have unwelcome visitors back here tonight."

He smiled at the anger and chagrin in her brown eyes, after which he turned slowly and stalked toward the big chair where Adam Tyrone waited in frowning silence. The old man had made no move to interfere, and Landon thought he detected a faint smile on the wise old face.

Several riders were seated on the benches along the wall, watching him with eyes that were hostile and suspicious. Landon stopped in front of the Mayor and removed his battered gray Stetson.

"I disobeyed your orders last night, Adam Tyrone," he began slowly. "Tiny Sutton and I rode across the sink, and into Paradise."

He could hear the startled gasp that ran around the hushed room. Eve Tyrone was coming forward, but Sutton stayed by the door. The old leader shook his head slowly and parted his bearded lips.

"Did I understand you to say that you rode into Paradise?"

Landon nodded. How much of his story would be believed was doubtful, but it was a story that would have to be told.

"Tiny Sutton heard Shawn O'Hara and his men talking," Landon said. "They rode into Paradise first."

"Keep on talking," Tyrone said harshly. "It was O'Hara's duty to guard the pass at both entrances!"

"I arrested two of them," Landon said clearly. "They were wanted by the Federal government."

He could feel the hush that fell over the big square room. The shifting of boots as men recovered from the surprise. Old Adam Tyrone spoke sharply.

"Then you are a lawman!"

Landon nodded his head. "Eve could have told you," he said quietly. "She found my badge the day she saved my life."

"Is this true?" Tyrone asked the girl sternly.

Eve Tyrone nodded. Her eyes were glittering with anger, and her lips curled at the corners when she glanced briefly at Landon.

"I found the badge," she admitted sullenly. "Perhaps I should have allowed Shawn O'Hara to carry out his first plan!"

Tyrone caught his breath sharply. His left hand started to stroke his white beard. A rough voice interrupted from the front door.

"Did you ever have the bottoms of your feet burned, old Adam?"

The old man straightened up and glared at Sutton. The little gunfighter stood with both hands close to his twin guns, his boots spaced wide for balance.

"This is not the time for riddles, Sutton," Tyrone said sternly, and then his face changed. "I trusted you, Tiny Sutton. To repay my trust, it seems that you have betrayed all of us!"

Sutton growled softly and cleared his throat. His slitted eyes wandered to the face of each Purgatory man. He smiled scornfully and made his answer.

"Being a man of peace, you wouldn't know much about killers," he said slowly. "Landon and I heard Grant Farnol make threats last night. It might be better for you to listen some more, and let Joel Landon do the talking!"

Adam Tyrone scowled, but something in Landon's face warned him. "We will listen," he said sullenly. "The floor is yours, Joel Landon!"

"You said O'Hara and his men were supposed to guard the pass," Landon began. "I am telling you they were working for Grant Farnol."

Tyrone leaned forward. "Do you mean that for Gospel truth?" he asked. "On your oath as a lawman?"

"I do," Landon said soberly. "O'Hara, O'Connor and Bocker were traitors to you. We heard them talking in Farnol's house in Paradise."

"And you were not discovered?"

"We slipped in through a hole under the house," Landon answered. "They did not know we were there."

"About my feet," Tyrone asked in a whisper, and he watched the thin face of Tiny Sutton.

"That old Indian gold mine that has been lost for years," Sutton answered evenly. "Farnol said you knew where it was. He said he would make you tell him, if he had to burn the bottoms of your feet!"

An angry murmur ran around the big room. Eve Tyrone turned pale and clenched her hands. Her lips parted as she stared at her grandfather, but the old patriarch nodded thoughtfully.

"I'd never tell if I knew," he declared firmly. "Why did you kill O'Hara and his men?"

"It was self defense, you might say," Landon answered. "Farnol told them to kill Tiny Sutton and me. They knew

67

that I represented the outside law, and O'Hara had orders to dig two new graves down there by the springs."

"Yours," Tyrone said just above his breath.

"Farnol is coming here tonight with all his men," Landon continued slowly. "Each of them will be deputized and will represent the law of Paradise."

"Tonight?" Tyrone whispered. "You said they were coming here tonight?"

"I said tonight," Landon answered soberly. "Shawn O'Hara and his men were to get your cattle for their part in betraying you to Farnol. Farnol wants both valleys back here, and that Indian gold mine. He controls all the law there is in Paradise, and his seizure would be considered legal."

Adam Tyrone rose slowly, came to Landon and extended his right hand. "Will you forgive an old fool?" he asked humbly.

Landon shook hands heartily. "I will," he answered. "You didn't know the whole story. Now every man in Purgatory will have to fight for what belongs to him."

"We'll fight!"

Husky voices shouted a battle-cry as hands slapped holsters. Then Whiskey Telford walked into the room, plucking nervously at his beard.

"I've got to have a drink," he said hoarsely, addressing Landon. "And I've important news."

Tiny Sutton handed Telford a small flask. The trembling doctor seized the bottle and emptied it without shame. The color returned to his pallid cheeks, and the tremble left his hands.

"I found it necessary to give Baldy Sanger some morphine so that I could probe and remove a bullet from his shoulder," Telford began. "Sanger began to talk not long ago. It would have been better if there had been just one reliable witness."

"Your word is good with me, Doctor Telford," Tyrone said gravely. "What did Sanger say?"

"Farnol means to kill every rider in Purgatory! He expects to ride in without opposition. With Sutton and Landon out of the way and O'Hara's men in control of the pass, the rest of you would have been slaughtered in your beds!"

Sutton tightened his lean jaw and stared at the faces of his fighting men. Telford shuddered and stared at Eve Tyrone.

"All were marked for death except the girl," he said hoarsely. "Farnol intends to keep her for his woman!"

Tyrone arose and held out a hand to stop the mutterings.

"Farnol would do this for gold," he said in a low voice. "You Purgatory men have heard the evidence. What is your decision?"

Silence for a moment, and then one young rider spoke in a clear ringing voice. "Tiny Sutton has the right idea. Shoot first, and ask questions later. Don't throw off your shots!"

The men nodded, and Tyrone spoke to Sutton. "My apologies to you, old friend," he said in his deep mellow voice. "A man never gets too old to learn."

All eyes watched as he opened a drawer in the desk. Tyrone took an old shell-studded belt, strapped it around his hips, and fastened the tie-backs low on his holster. Then he slipped the heavy gun a time or two to get the feel of the smooth wood.

"Grant Farnol will find us ready," Tyrone stated clearly. "Thanks to Sutton and Joel Landon. Will you lead us, Landon?"

"There are about twenty in their party," Landon said. "We have twelve men. Farnol has branded you all as outlaws. Now I am asking you all to hold up your right hands, and take the oath of loyalty to the Federal government!"

10

A DEEP SILENCE held briefly, and then every hand in the Council room went up. Joel Landon spoke the oath of office in a clear voice, and Eve Tyrone was the first to answer.

"I do!"

Joel Landon showed his weariness for the first time. He had ridden all night across Hell's Basin. He had had no sleep, and it was almost noon. He turned to the door slowly.

"Get your rifles ready, men. Guard the pass at both ends. I mean to catch a little sleep while I can. Come on, Tiny."

They left the big room and walked to their weary horses. Sutton stopped at his cabin; Landon rode on to his own. He stripped his riding gear and turned the animal into a corral, ladled a measure of grain, and stacked the manger deep with prairie hay. Then Landon shuffled to his cabin and pulled off his dusty boots. He threw himself on the low bed with a sigh of satisfaction. All his muscles were relaxed until a shadow fell across the doorsill. He frowned when Eve Tyrone came in and seated herself on the edge of the bed.

"I had to come, Joel," she said gently. "Because of the things I said, and the things I thought about you, I might have shot you, after all you have done for us."

"You wouldn't have shot," Landon murmured drowsily. "Now I want to get some sleep."

"Am I nothing more to you than that?" Eve asked softly.

Landon's senses were drugged with fatigue. "That's about all," he muttered gruffly. "I came up here to do a job of work, and women don't fit in with the kind of work I do."

His voice was harsh and edgy with strain and weariness. Eve sighed and released his big hand. She watched while he stretched and opened his mouth to yawn like a small boy. His right hand was close to the gun in his holster, and his lean fighting jaw was set like a shoulder of granite.

Eve remembered his blistered skin and torn hands after his long walk across the desert—without water. Landon was in a deep sleep, and she stared at him with silent fascination. Her voice was a low whisper when she murmured to herself.

"I could die for a man like ... ?"

Landon stirred and clutched at his left side. Eve saw the caked blood on the shirt, but Landon was drugged with sleep. She leaned down and brushed his lips lightly with her own. A pan of water stood on a window sill in the hot sun. The girl found a cloth, gently opened the sleeping man's shirt, and bathed the wound. Her fingers touched his breast and felt the strong steady beat of his heart. She covered him with a light blanket, and then her arms went about him, and she held him to her rounded breasts like a mother holds her child. Landon murmured in his sleep and buried his face in the rounded hollow of her shoulder. Then she was on her feet when a scraping boot warned that someone was coming. It was Tiny Sutton.

"He is asleep now," she said. "You can't disturb him."

"I know it," Sutton said roughly. "I just came over to ride you off so that he could bed down and get his rest. I want to talk some to you, Eve. About something important."

Eve Tyrone closed her eyes. Her shoulders trembled, and Sutton patted her shoulder. "Take it easy, gal," he whispered.

"Come over to my cabin. You can tell old Tiny anything you got on your mind."

"Tiny," she whispered huskily at Sutton's cabin, "I almost die when he looks at me as though I were one of the riding hands. I'm just another man to him!"

"Sure you are," Sutton agreed. "That big feller has a heap of work to do. Right now he's the Federal government, little gal. It ain't like you to go on the prod this way."

Eve nodded through her tears. She was tall and strong, deep-breasted to tell of her mountain blood. Now she felt like a little girl, and she clung to Sutton's gnarled hand.

"He saved all of us," she said shakily. "And I thought he was working for Grant Farnol. He will never forgive me for what I said."

"He ain't even thinking about you," Sutton answered bluntly. "If you could have seen Farnol's face when he was talking about burning old Adam's feet, mebbe you'd know how Landon feels!"

The girl shuddered. "I know," she whispered. "Then I remembered taking the gun away from Joel. He might have been killed!"

"Don't fret about it, Eve," Sutton said. "Men don't think like women when it comes to a fight. But you did put Joel in a bad way with Limpy Bocker getting ready to pull a sneak."

"I was a fool," Eve admitted. "He won't ever forget."

"Landon is a gunfighter," Sutton reminded. "He's the fastest man I have ever seen. You did something big when you saved his life, and like you just said, Joel won't ever forget."

"I'm afraid of Grant Farnol now," the girl admitted. "I'd kill myself if he ever caught me."

"Quit that shaking," Sutton barked. "First time I ever knowed you to get scared since you was a long-legged filly. You're forgetting that Jesse Tyrone was your Dad. Now you take a brace on yourself and get ready to fight!"

"I'm ashamed of myself, Tiny. From now on I'll fight like the rest of the Purgatory riders."

"That's talking like a man," Sutton praised, and then he smiled. "But you won't act like a man after the deputy marshal finishes the job he came here to do," he added confidently.

"Tiny," the girl pleaded, "don't you ever mention a word of what I've said."

Sutton huffed up and scowled. "Did you ever know me to go around with a slack jaw?" he asked roughly.

"I was all wrong," the girl murmured. "You trusted Joel Landon from the minute you first saw him."

"You can tell a heap about a man by what you see behind his eyes," the little gunfighter said earnestly. "You used to be right good at reading sign, Eve."

"I don't understand."

"Sure you do," Sutton argued. "There's many a time in these old hills where a feller don't stop to ask fool questions. He just follows his conscience, or whatever it is that points the way he ought to go."

"I feel better now, Tiny."

"Good. Now you high-tail and let me get some sleep. Call me and Joel for a late supper, and make the coffee plenty strong."

Eve Tyrone walked away with a light step. Sutton watched her for a moment and then sought his bed.

"Landon won't always have work on his mind," he said with a chuckle. He undressed and went to bed, and was asleep almost instantly. The hours of the afternoon ticked away while the two men slept soundly.

Joel Landon stirred restlessly when a soft knock sounded on his door. He awoke clear-eyed and with every sense alert, his right hand on his gun.

"Who is it?"

The door opened slowly and Adam Tyrone entered. A different Adam with the old gun-belt sagging on his hips, the tie-backs thonged low on his sturdy leg. He was more like an ancient Viking leader than the peaceful stock-raiser.

"We have set our trap, Joel," Tyrone began heavily. "I have waited long for the coming of the real law. The right is on our side; it always has been."

"See that every man has plenty of ammunition," Landon said grimly. "I doubt if they will make much work for Doc Telford."

"Speaking of Telford," Tyrone changed the subject quickly. "Because I do not use strong drink myself, it was difficult for me to understand what Telford was suffering. I am thankful that you did."

"Telford is different from most of us," Landon said gravely. "His training has developed his imagination more than his muscular system, and his nerves are the first to feel the strain of the work he does."

"I know," Tyrone agreed. "With your help, he will overcome his weakness."

"I'm counting on it," Landon answered seriously. "There will be work for him before this night is done."

"We will station our men on both walls of the pass," Tyrone said quietly. "When the raiders ride through, we will call on them to throw down their arms and surrender. The law says that every man must be given a chance!"

Landon turned with disbelief reflected in his features. He knew the ruthless plans of Grant Farnol.

"You tell me that after all you know about Farnol?" he asked. "Do you really believe they will surrender?"

"I say it because I know Farnol," Tyrone answered. "When he sees there is no chance, he will surrender unconditionally."

"You are trying to see Farnol through your own mind," Landon said curtly. "You would think of your people before yourself. Farnol is a different breed. He would sacrifice every man in his band to gain his own desires and would count the cost as trifling!"

"I cannot believe that any man would do such a thing," Tyrone argued stubbornly. "With all his men under our guns, Farnol will have no alternative."

"Farnol would continue the fight if he had to do it alone," Landon said shortly. "He knows what it would mean to be taken alive, and to understand him thoroughly, you would have to put yourself in his place."

"That I have tried to do while you were taking a much-needed rest," the old man said patiently. "You represent the outside law which is bigger than any individual, or group. Farnol knows that this law represents the entire forces of the United States."

"He does not recognize any law except that which he makes," Landon contradicted, but he knew his arguments were futile.

He did not attempt to reason with the old patriarch. They walked outside into the gloom of twilight. Wood smoke was billowing up from a big open fireplace behind the Council building. Most of the Purgatory men were eating. Every man was armed with rifle and six-shooter, and eating in silence as working cowboys do.

Eve Tyrone brought a plate of steaming food and placed it on the long table before Landon. She smiled when he thanked her pleasantly. Tiny Sutton had just finished his meal. The little gunfighter winked at Landon when Tyrone cleared his throat to address the men.

"We are not killers," he began quietly. "The enemy will

73

attack some time after midnight, beyond a doubt. You men are all sworn to an oath, and Farnol's men must have a chance to surrender!"

Tiny Sutton frowned and cleared his throat. "You are wrong this time, Adam," he contradicted. "At one time or another, I've arrested every man in Farnol's pack of wolves. Those men won't surrender!"

Tyrone frowned as he faced his men. Most of them had been raised in the rugged hills where a man did a day's work when he reached the age of fifteen. They had suffered the stigma of outlawry for five years, but now they sensed that liberation was near.

"They will surrender," Tyrone declared positively. "Even Farnol knows that he cannot beat the outside law. Joel Landon will speak him fair—before a shot is fired from our side!"

Landon stared down at his plate. His size and breadth of shoulder was matched by nearly every man in the crowd. Only old Adam was bigger and Landon now faced the kindly face of the man of peace.

"They get a chance to surrender," he admitted reluctantly. "That is the way of the law."

He heard Sutton growl deep in his throat. The little gunfighter pushed to the front and took his stand beside Landon.

"Like he says, boys," he agreed harshly. "We all made a promise when Landon made us a part of the law. That's the biggest difference between Farnol's men and us."

Landon knew the effort it had required for Sutton to back him up. Sutton was a killer by his own admission, but he had also carried the law for many years.

"Landon calls on Farnol's men to throw down their hardware," Sutton continued. "While he is going through that legal formality, the rest of us each picks out a killer and lines him under our sights center. We all cut loose when one of those curly wolves stampedes and fires the first shot!"

Landon nodded vigorously. "That's the law, men," he agreed. "The law also gives every man the right to protect himself."

"We can kill the horses as an act of mercy," the old man suggested hopefully. "It will save many human lives."

"Those horses don't know any better, but their riders do," Sutton said hoarsely. "I'm telling you again that they won't give up their guns. Now you get that straight, Adam Tyrone!"

Landon nodded in confirmation. "You and Eve should stay

74

up in the valley," he said. "This is work for fighting men who know how, and who want to fight!"

"Which includes us," Eve answered without hesitation. "You can count on us, Joel Landon."

Landon smiled grimly. He had no doubt about the girl, but Adam Tyrone had been a man of peace for many years. Fixed habits in the aged are hard to change.

The riders from Purgatory reached the pass after darkness had fallen.

Sutton leaned forward and stared intently across the star-studded desert. He spoke jerkily.

"Riders coming, Joel. I'm getting back to pass the word to our men. I'll be back to help with the reception!"

Sutton jumped his horse and sped up through the twisting pass.

Landon could see a long line of bobbing hats sky-lined against the white sand. Grant Farnol was riding to Purgatory with his killers!

"Get down behind those rocks," he ordered sternly. "Don't make a sound until every man is in the pass. I'll do the talking!"

Tyrone nodded and crossed over to take his position behind a shoulder of rock. The girl stayed with Landon, watching the ghostly riders looming larger in the eerie moonlight. Sutton rounded a turn in the pass with three riders, and Landon waved them to positions.

"Not a sound," he warned. "We want every man to get into the pass before they know we are here. The slightest noise will spoil our surprise and will cost many lives!"

They could hear the faint voices of the raiders when the advancing column left the protection of the row of tombstones. Landon counted twenty-two horses, and his eyes hardened when he recognized the bulk of Grant Farnol. The big gambler was giving quiet orders, secure in the belief that Shawn O'Hara and his men were guarding the pass.

Sutton crouched behind a rock and raised his rifle. He lined his sights on the big man in the black broadcloth. Not more than thirty yards away now. Then a booming voice broke the stillness of the desert night.

"Surrender in the name of the law, Grant Farnol!"

Landon recognized the voice of old Adam Tyrone. Sutton swore viciously and tripped the trigger under his finger. Eve Tyrone knocked Sutton to one side as he tried to lever another shell into the breech of his smoking rifle.

75

The raiders in the pass spurred their horses and fired their guns as they raced across the rocky floor.

Sutton freed himself from the girl. His six-shooters began to roar as the men of Purgatory found the range and began cutting down the odds against them.

Landon was watching Farnol who was out on the desert floor. He squinted down his rifle barrel and slowly squeezed the trigger. He smiled grimly when the horse went down in full stride, pitching Farnol into the shadow of protecting rocks.

"Try that journey of death yourself," he muttered.

"You would do that to a man after what you went through?" a husky voice asked angrily, and Eve Tyrone stared at Landon.

"Because of what I went through," Landon corrected. "And because old Adam spoiled our plans!"

"You would have killed all those men for personal revenge?" the girl asked in a horrified whisper.

Landon laughed bitterly. "Are you forgetting the women up in the village?" he asked. "And that Farnol's men have us out-numbered?"

Landon jerked around when the girl clutched his arm. A horse broke away from the rocks on the opposite side of the pass. Sparks spattered under its shod hooves, and then the animal raced out on the desert floor. A tall white-bearded man sat at the saddle erect, urging the horse toward the place where Farnol had taken refuge. Bullets whined about the erect figure, but Adam Tyrone rode like a man with a mission.

Landon levered a shell into the breech of his rifle. Farnol would kill Tyrone, take his horse and escape. He saw the girl reaching toward him as he clicked the hammer back. His left hand darted out and threw her to one side. He leaped clear of the rocks with the rifle ready.

Adam Tyrone was half-way across the desert floor when the gun barked flatly. The big racing horse lifted high in a mighty leap and then crashed to the sand.

"You did that to Gramps!" Eve Tyrone screamed. "You killed him!"

"I shot his horse to save him," Landon said roughly. "Farnol meant to kill him and take the horse!"

Eve stared at the still figure of the old patriarch. "You shot the horse?" she whispered. "You said the horse?"

"Joel got that horse dead center," Tiny Sutton shouted angrily. "Farnol shot at Adam at the same time."

"He's all I have," the girl whispered, and she started for the clearing.

Landon grabbed her by the arms. The girl fought to free herself. Landon tightened his arms and held her close.

Sutton glared at the struggling girl, and then he shouted at Landon. "She's out of her head, Joel. We better tie her up to keep her from getting killed. She will head straight for the old man if we turn her loose, and Grant Farnol will get her."

11

LANDON SPOKE QUIETLY.

"Take her back to the women. I'm going to try to get Adam."

"You're going out there to make a target of yourself?" Sutton asked.

"Perhaps not so much of a target," Landon replied. "The clouds are coming in. In ten minutes or less it will be pitch dark. I'm going to try. You get Eve out of here. The women can handle her better than we can."

Sutton shook his head doubtfully. Then he forgot sentiment when he raised the girl's face and studied her. She was making little moaning noises through tightly clenched teeth. Guns flamed from both sides of the pass as Sutton made ready for the dangerous ride.

Landon removed his spurs and tightened his belt. He cuffed the wide-brimmed hat down over his eyes after a look at the black clouds coming in over the towering Vermillion Cliffs. He crouched down behind the rocks of Dripping Springs and measured the distance to the dead horse.

The animal was lying on the desert floor, halfway between himself and the hiding place of Grant Farnol. There was no sign of life or movement to disturb the ghostly isolation of the tombstones, but Landon knew that death was lurking in the tall shadows.

Sutton climbed his saddle. Landon picked up the girl and laid her across the pommel, face down. The firing stopped, and the little gunman rode up the pass in a silence that seemed magnified after the roaring battle.

The light became hazier, and then the clouds rolled slowly to blot out the moonlight. Landon ran swiftly across the rocks toward the horse he had killed.

The exact location was in his mind. He ran blindly through the darkness, counting his steps. A few paces and his outstretched hand touched leather. Tyrone would be a few feet to the right. Landon grunted softly when his fingers touched a big body.

He jerked back when a pair of sinewy hands clutched his shoulders and tightened down on his arms. Old Adam possessed no such strength. Landon realized he had found Grant Farnol.

A mountain of brawn fell on top of him and bore him down to the shifting sands. He twisted sideways just as a pair of incredibly powerful arms wrapped around him and drew him close. It was like the jaws of a bear trap clamping together to imprison him, and Landon knew he would have to act fast.

He brought up both knees in a jackknife movement before the trap could close. Then he kicked with all the strength of his long legs to catapult the heavy body into space. Clutching fingers tore at his shirt and bruised the skin of his arms, but he was free again, and struggling to his feet.

A gun blazed suddenly, and Landon felt the whistling bullet fan his left cheek. His own right hand whipped down to his holster instinctively. His gun came up slashing flame and powder at the figure just dodging behind the first rock in the long row.

"Let him go, son. He has chosen the journey of death!"

Landon stopped abruptly. The voice belonged to Adam Tyrone.

"Are you hurt bad, old-timer?"

"My head hurts, Joel. I'm sorry for being a stubborn old fool. We all pay for our mistakes."

Landon knew what it meant for Tyrone to abandon his program of peace. He found the old man and pulled him to his feet.

"That pays the bill, Adam Tyrone," he whispered. "We better start back to the village."

Landon heard hoofbeats coming toward the waterhole. One of the cowboys was evidently riding out to lend a

78

hand. He frowned when the horse passed on the right and raced away in the darkness.

"I've got him!" he shouted. "Circle on back here and lend me a hand!"

No answer came from the horseman. Landon slapped for his six-shooter and fanned back the hammer with his thumb. He stopped his trigger finger just in time. He lowered the weapon with a sigh, telling himself that only a fool would throw lead blindly. The rider might be either a Purgatory cowboy or an outlaw.

Tyrone was standing with legs spread wide for balance. Landon helped him to the water-hole. The clouds rolled back just as they came to Dripping Springs. Landon stared when four Purgatory riders came forward with rifles in their grimy hands. Every gun came up when the cowboys saw the two figures on foot. They lowered again when the men recognized Landon and Tyrone.

"Who was that rider who just bolted out through the pass?" Landon asked the leading cowboy. "He busted out there across the sink, and he was heading for Paradise from the sounds of his horse."

"We thought it was Sutton, and we held our fire," the cowboy answered. "Are you hurt bad, Mayor Tyrone?" he asked the old man.

Tyrone grunted and asked a question of his own. "Where's Eve?"

The four cowboys crowded around and stared with mouths open. They glanced at each other, and the tall Jud asked the question that was in every mind.

"You mean she's gone? She ain't down here at the Springs with you and Landon?"

"Tiny took her back to Purgatory," Landon answered, and then he stiffened with a sudden thought. "Did I hear shooting up yonder in the pass?" he asked.

"There were two shots," the cowboy answered. "That ought to just about finish up them four killers who rode through first. The ones who were in before the Mayor called to Grant Farnol."

Landon and Tyrone turned slowly and stared at each other. Tyrone began to sag. Landon spoke to Jud Farrel who had dismounted.

"Take care of old Adam. I'm riding ahead to find Tiny Sutton!"

He leaped for his horse, catching up the trailing reins

with his left hand. Then he was in the saddle, spurring madly for the gooseneck, up through the twisting pass in the pale moonlight, riding his spurs to get every bit of speed from the sure-footed mountain horse.

He reigned in sharply when he rounded a bend and saw three men leaning over a fourth. He was out of the saddle and on the ground before the horse had stopped, pushing one of the men aside.

"Tiny!" Landon whispered softly, and he went to his knees to grip the little gunfighter by both shoulders. "Did they get you bad, pard?"

"Naw," Sutton lied gamely, and he tried to sit up. "But he got Eve, Joel. He dry-gulched me from the rocks when I rode through, and I must have hit my head on a rock when I fell out of my old kak. I'm all right now, marshal. You fork my horse and take on out after that damn killer!"

Landon gripped Sutton's hand and nodded. His eyes were blazing with anger, and his voice was thick when he ripped out a low question.

"Where's Doc Telford? We need him right away!"

"That's him over yonder with his black satchel," Jud answered, and he pointed to a tall figure coming from behind a cropping of rocks. "We got three men back there when they first rode through, and Doc tried to find one he could patch up. He was wasting his time, because none of us threw off our shots."

The doctor arrived just in time to hear the last remark. "All dead," he murmured, and then he saw Tiny Sutton. "Here's a man who needs my help." He went to his knees and opened the black bag.

Landon watched for a moment. Then he slipped away to his horse. He knew that it would be impossible to track either Farnol or the escaped raider who was out in Hell's Basin with the delirious girl. Both would try to make their way back to Paradise. Landon squared his shoulders and made his decision.

Adam Tyrone stopped him at the edge of Dripping Springs. The Purgatory cowboys were making the rounds to make sure that all the Paradise killers were incapable of further treachery. Tyrone spoke shakily.

"Eve?" he whispered. "Is she . . .?"

Landon did not reproach the old leader who had spoiled all his careful plans. He stared into the pleading gray eyes when he found his voice and answered quietly.

"Only one man besides Grant Farnol. Right now that man is taking Eve across Hell's Basin to Paradise!"

"You must be wrong," Tyrone said jerkily. Landon turned his face to avoid the hopeless expression on the old patriarch's face.

"You remember that horse we heard cutting over there to the right?" he reminded grimly. "That was the man who shot Tiny Sutton from his saddle. He has Eve in front of him out there."

"And I did that," Tyrone whispered brokenly. "I sacrificed my own flesh and blood, because I wanted to spare those who came to kill us. I will never forgive myself!"

"I'm riding," Landon said gruffly, and he filled his canteen at the water-hole. "I'll be back!"

Tyrone stared for a long moment, and then his tall frame drew erect in the moonlight. "I will go with you," he announced bravely, but his voice held a broken note of despair.

Landon shook his head and tightened his cinches. The horse had drunk deeply, and was blowing softly while it keened the night air coming in from the desert.

"He rides fastest who rides alone," Landon reminded soberly. "You stay back here and look after Tiny Sutton. He was hurt pretty bad, and he got it trying to save Eve. You owe it to Tiny."

"Doctor Telford will take care of Sutton," Tyrone argued desperately, but his square shoulders drooped with weariness and despair. The weight of his years was heavy upon him.

"You would only slow me down, Adam," Landon said gently. "You stay here, and have the boys do what is necessary before the sun gets high."

He pointed to the sprawling bodies of the outlaw dead to make his meaning clear. The Purgatory riders followed his pointing finger, and slowly nodded their heads. Adam Tyrone shuddered and closed his eyes. His trembling lips moved in silent prayer.

"We will do the needful, Joel," one of the cowboys said gravely. "Are you sure you don't want some of us to ride along with you?"

"Certain," Landon answered shortly. "I know the desert better than most, and my best chance lies in moving quietly, and counting on a bit of luck. It's about time I had some, and you boys will have all the work to do here."

"You've done more than your share," Jud Farrel said quietly. "But you're the boss."

Adam Tyrone watched Landon make his simple preparations, and his eyes seemed weak and faded now. The Purgatory men started clearing the ground back from the waterhole, singing softly while they worked, as though they were riding circle around their sleeping herds of cattle.

Landon watched them for a moment, and then climbed his saddle. The moon was waning in the sky and moving closer to the scud of drifting clouds. Landon laid a hand on Tyrone's shoulder and spoke quietly.

"I should be back sometime after daybreak, Adam. If I don't turn up about then, bring every rider in Purgatory and lead them into Paradise."

"Into Paradise?" Tyrone repeated slowly. "You said for us to ride into Paradise, Joel?"

"Farnol's power is broken now," Landon said confidently. "We will strike before he has time to gather another band around him. There are many good citizens in Paradise, and they will welcome you back home. I'm sure of it."

The old man reached up and gripped Landon's hand. "Eve," he whispered shakily. "You will do all you can, Joel Landon. *Vaya con Dios!*"

"Go thou with God," Landon repeated the Spanish blessing softly, and he nodded his head. "Thank you, Adam Tyrone."

Landon rode off through the shifting sand with a watchful eye for the trail of the running horse. Once he raised his head and smiled grimly at the row of tall tombstones across the arid wasteland. Grant Farnol was out there somewhere, and when the sun came up?

A knot of muscle tightened in his stomach as he thought of the girl. Eve Tyrone was a beautiful girl, big and strong. Landon frowned in the semi-darkness. He wondered about her strength, and the weight of worry that had caused her mind to slip. A brief rest might have restored her, but now she was out there in the desert, at the mercy of an outlaw.

The moon dipped down behind the high serrated peaks of the Vermillion Cliffs. Darkness descended upon the desert like a velvety cloak, and a cool breeze blew down from the north. The hardy horse moved forward at a steady dog-trot, leaving the miles behind. The wind soon covered the tracks, as it had wiped out all trace of the rider who had shot Tiny Sutton.

82

The knot tightened in the belly of the tall deputy marshal. Tiny Sutton and Eve Tyrone, the two people to whom he owed the most. His hand touched the grips of his pistol, and somehow it eased the gripping torment in his stomach. He remembered the wish of Adam Tyrone. Go thou with God!

12

THREE HOURS PASSED, and then Joel Landon saw a bobbing dot skylined on the rim of the desert. One rider was in the saddle, with another man walking beside the tiring horse. Paradise would be up ahead. Landon grunted softly and turned toward the south where a distant clump of desert willows marked the house of Grant Farnol. Only the light of the stars filtered down to cast a hazy glow. Landon swung down and tied his sweating horse behind the deserted house. He stood quiet for a time, listening to catch any vagrant sound.

A moment later he was making his way toward the back door, and he tested his weight carefully on every step when he climbed to the small porch. The door knob turned under his fingers, and no one challenged his silent passage through the kitchen.

He stopped in the big front room and struck a match between his cupped hands. He heard the soft clop of hooves when he lighted a coal-oil lamp and turned the wick low. Then he twitched his gun to make sure it would not hang, and seated himself at the table facing the front door, in the same chair where Grant Farnol had given orders for his death.

Footsteps came up the rough stairs and slithered across the porch floor. The door was thrown open suddenly. Eve Tyrone was pushed into the room with her hands thonged behind her back. Her shoulders were sagging with weariness when she stopped and waited for her captor.

Landon tugged his gray Stetson low over his eyes and peered from under the sheltering brim. He caught his breath sharply when a wide-shouldered giant pushed the girl ahead of him and closed the door. The man had red hair and a heavy red beard.

For a moment Landon thought he was seeing Shawn O'Hara, and then the red giant turned and faced the light. He was younger than Shawn by five years, and his step was as light as a panther's when he crossed the room. Landon pushed back his hat and waited for the man to speak.

"I figured you'd be here, Chief," he began, and then stopped suddenly when he discovered his mistake.

Landon waved his right hand and spoke softly. His gun was ready for a shot.

"You're covered, Mister. I'd say that you were kin to Shawn O'Hara, so don't move sudden unless you want to join him!"

Eve Tyrone stepped forward at the sound of the deputy marshal's voice. She stopped abruptly when Landon barked a sharp order.

"Stay where you are, Eve!"

The red giant crouched forward with his little eyes blazing savagely. Landon came to his feet, his gun spiking from his big fist. Then the stranger snarled viciously.

"I'm Rory O'Hara, brother to Shawn. I'll get you, Landon!"

All his life Landon had studied men. He knew that the big outlaw was going to take a chance. Rory O'Hara was going to match his draw against Landon's drop.

"Don't try it," Landon warned just above his breath. "You wouldn't have a chance!"

Rory O'Hara growled deep in his throat. His big boots were spaced wide, and he slapped down suddenly with his right hand. Landon's gun roared like sullen thunder, and the explosion echoed against the low ceiling like a distant storm.

O'Hara's clutching fingers pawed air at the place on his belt where his holster had hung a scant second ago. Then he hurled his big body toward the smoking gun with a smothered curse of rage ripping from his twisted lips. Landon tightened his lips and slipped the hammer under his calloused thumb.

The heavy slug caught the rushing giant in the right shoulder and spun him into a turn. He stamped one big boot to right himself. Joel Landon stepped forward and struck once with the heavy barrel of his smoking forty-five. The big man thudded to the worn planking.

For a moment he watched the younger O'Hara with the gun held ready in his hand. Then he turned slowly and

84

caught his breath with surprise when he saw the expression of loathing on Eve Tyrone's stained face.

"Killer!" she whispered hoarsely. "Don't touch me!"

Landon ejected the spent shells from his gun for something to do. He reloaded while he studied her thoughtfully. He remembered the hysteria back at Dripping Springs when Tiny Sutton had carried the girl up the pass toward Purgatory. Now her brown eyes seemed normal. He shrugged while his right hand slowly holstered his gun.

He crossed the room when he saw a short rope lying in one corner. The girl watched suspiciously when he caught up the rope and made a loop around the outlaw's right wrist. Landon ignored her while he tied the big hands tightly, after which he seated himself in Grant Farnol's chair by the table.

Eve Tyrone was leaning forward, staring at the red-bearded outlaw. Her breasts were heaving when she turned to Landon with a startled gleam widening her dark eyes.

"You didn't kill him," she whispered tensely. "I thought you had shot him down in cold blood. Your face was so hard and merciless, and it all seemed like a terrible dream!"

"It was a nightmare," Landon corrected dryly. "For a while I thought that I was seeing the ghost of Shawn O'Hara."

"Joel," the girl sobbed suddenly. "Please look at me. Please talk to me!"

"Sure," the deputy marshal muttered. "I'd do more than talk to you if you were a man. You took it on yourself to spoil most of my plans tonight, but it did little good."

His voice was hard and uncompromising, to match the flinty look in his eyes. His face was like a craggy shoulder of granite, and the girl stared at him, her lips parted.

Landon kept his eyes averted because he did not know what to do. Should he free her now? Had she fully recovered her mind?

"Farnol?" Eve repeated slowly. "Where is he?"

"Heading for Paradise," Landon answered coldly. "He is out there in Hell's Basin on foot!"

The girl stared while she tried to remember the events of the night. Her eyes narrowed, and she leaned forward and whispered jerkily.

"Grandfather. Is he dead? I saw him fall."

"Old Adam is safe," Landon said shortly. "Tiny Sutton was badly wounded, trying to get you to safety when you lost your head and went on a stampede."

"Tiny hurt?" and the girl shook her head slowly. "I don't remember about him taking me away from the springs."

"He put you in front of his saddle," Landon explained. "This Rory O'Hara shot Tiny from ambush. He was bringing you here to Grant Farnol. I rode across by the short-cut, and got here first to welcome him home."

The girl lowered her head and bit her full red lips. She came to Landon and looked him squarely in the eyes.

"I am quite all right now," she said quietly. "Will you please release my hands? The thongs are cutting off the circulation."

He nodded and reached in his pocket for his stock knife. He severed the rawhide thongs and watched while she rubbed her wrists in an effort to restore the circulation. His eyes squinted thoughtfully as he reviewed the events of the night. The girl shuddered when she read his thoughts.

"Saying that I am sorry won't bring those dead men back to life," she murmured. "I can see it all now. Many of them would have surrendered if I hadn't pushed Tiny's rifle aside. They would have been helpless without a leader. I did it without thinking when Grandfather shouted for them to surrender."

Landon nodded soberly. He made no answer, and after a pause the girl spoke again in a low hopeless tone.

"I thought you had lost your temper and had deliberately killed Gramps when he rode out after Farnol," she admitted frankly. "Gramps never moved after his horse went down."

"I shot the horse from under him," Landon said grimly. "Farnol meant to kill old Adam and take the horse to make his own escape. I was determined that he should know the hell of that journey of death!"

His eyes met her squarely. The girl shuddered at the cold determination she saw in those narrowed gray eyes. The first light of dawn filtered through the high window, and Landon slowly shook his head.

"You will not interfere this time," he told her firmly. "A strong man can make that trip across Hell's Basin, before the sun gets too hot. Farnol is a very strong man!"

"But when the sun comes up," the girl protested. "You know all too well what that means."

"I do," Landon said grimly. "Farnol will have four, perhaps five hours in that hell where he has sent so many other men. The law will be waiting for him when he finishes *El Jornado de Muerte*. If he does finish it," he added.

Eve Tyrone forgot herself. She watched the hard face of the desert man for some sign of pity. Landon was watching the rising dawn through the high window, and the girl shook her head.

"I can't bear to think of it," she whispered. "Is there no other way, Joel?"

Landon turned slowly with his head lowered. The dust of the desert powdered her clothing, and his jaw tightened when he saw the angry red welts on her wrists.

"Have you forgotten what Baldy Sanger said about Farnol wanting you?" he asked. "And that Farnol has the reputation of getting what he wants?"

"You'd torture him for that?"

"No!" Landon's answer was an emphatic denial.

"You did this for me," Eve murmured. "You rode across Hell's Basin to save me from him."

Again Landon shook his head stubbornly. "I did it for the people of Purgatory," he corrected bluntly. "For the men and women who have been exiled back there for more than five years. I did it because I represent the law which is supposed to protect all decent citizens, regardless of who they might be!"

"You are hard, Joel Landon," the girl said reproachfully. "I suppose one gets that way when he rides for the law. Tiny Sutton is the same kind of a man."

"I reckon that's the answer," the deputy marshal agreed.

The man on the floor stirred restlessly and tried to sit up. Landon propped the big shoulders against the wall, and stood back to watch and wait. Rory O'Hara shook his red head and opened his little eyes with a groan. He glared like a wild boar at bay.

"Farnol will get you for this, you damn star-toter," he growled hoarsely. "You got me on a sneak, just like you done for Shawn. You didn't have the sand to make it an even break!"

"And you jumped the gun," Landon said slowly. "You are not in any position to talk about sneaks. You didn't give Tiny Sutton any warning when you shot him out of his saddle, and you were hiding behind a rock when you did it."

"I'm glad I killed that runty lawman," O'Hara said viciously. "Farnol missed him one time, but I don't miss."

"Tiny Sutton is not dead," Landon corrected. "Tiny will get well in time to watch you hang."

"I won't hang," O'Hara boasted, but his shoulders sagged.

"Perhaps you want to talk before I take you to Slag City," Landon suggested. "All your pards are dead, and Farnol won't waste any tears on them."

Rory O'Hara set his big jaw. "I'm ready to go," he grunted. "I'd rather take that *pasear* across the sink than face Farnol after falling down on my job."

Deputy Smiley came into the room, glanced at Eve Tyrone and walked over to take a good look at the wounded prisoner.

"He's brother to the late Shawn O'Hara," Landon explained. "He shot Tiny Sutton. Take him to Slag City right away and book him on that charge while you look up his record. Tell the Chief I ought to be back within a week if my plans work out."

"OK, Joel," Smiley answered. "Are you wanting any help now, or playing it lone-handed?"

Landon glanced at Eve and shook his head.

"I have all the help I need, Smiley," Landon said quietly. "Take Rory out, and I'll be seeing you soon."

Landon went back into the room and shut the door after him. Eve Tyrone had stretched out on the couch, her eyes closed. Landon smiled when he saw the gun close to her right hand. Eve would take care of herself now. He tiptoed out through the kitchen.

Landon allowed his horse a scanty drink, filled his canteen and rode off at a walk.

Paradise was a cluster of buildings more than a mile away. Smiley and his prisoner were a pair of tiny dots far to the south. Landon walked his horse slowly across the desert floor.

The sun climbed high and sent forth radiations of scorching heat. It was ten o'clock when Landon glanced at his watch—time enough for a strong man to have crossed most of the strip if he knew the short cuts.

Landon's lips tightened when he saw a circling dot high above, floating lazily on motionless wings. Another dot joined the first. He lowered his head and stared intently at the desert floor under the circling carrion birds.

A crawling figure left the shade of the last rock and started across the blinding stretch toward the desert willows. The man's black broadcloth trousers hung in shreds about his legs, and his boots left a pair of ruts in the sand behind him.

Landon sat on his horse and watched the crawling man with no sign of pity on his craggy face. Grant Farnol was getting back a bit of his own.

13

LANDON SENT his horse closer, then reined in and sat his saddle to watch and wait.

Farnol reached for his gun and thumbed three shots at the dodging horse which Landon neck-reined from side to side to present an erratic target. Little jets of sand spouted up around the horse, and the explosions came belatedly after each shot.

The big gambler stared at his smoking gun and reached to his belt. Thumb and finger closed around his last cartridge. White teeth clenched grimly when the bullet was passed through the loading gate. Then Joel Landon laughed mockingly.

The crawling man snarled like a bear infuriated beyond all endurance. His hand jerked out with finger pressing the trigger. He saw the spurt of sand that signaled a miss. Then he crumpled down and fought against the dizziness that fogged his tortured brain.

Landon waited and watched with a curious sense of detachment he could not have explained. He knew every feeling of the man who had sent him on the dreaded journey of death. He remembered the boasts of the gambler concerning those other men who had died and had been left for the coyotes and the buzzards.

His face softened some when Farnol raised himself on hands and knees and crawled a few steps. Then his face hardened when he remembered the men back in Purgatory— men who had died that this selfish monster might live and carry on his inhuman plans.

Landon's hand moved toward the canteen on his saddle when Farnol crawled a few more steps and collapsed in the shifting sand. The desert man waited and slowly shook his head until the gambler roused himself to move again.

Three crawling steps. A long rest. Two steps the next time. Then only one.

Landon sent his horse toward the sprawling bulk and swung down with pity in his gray eyes. He had sworn to watch Grant Farnol suffer as he had made so many other men suffer on the terrible journey of death. But Landon could find no satisfaction in the spectacle while he looked down at the groveling man in the blistering sand.

Five hours under the blazing sun had almost finished Grant Farnol. His tongue was blackened and swollen, sagging from his big mouth. His fingers were raw and bleeding where he had tried to claw a hold in the shifting sands of old man desert.

Some men fight the desert; others go with it. Joel Landon was a desert man, now he acted like one.

He went to his knees and removed the neckerchief from Farnol's throat. He soaked the cloth in cool water from the canteen. His hands moved slowly when he hunkered down beside the huge body and wrapped the swollen tongue in the moistened cloth. A very little water would kill the gambler now, but his tissues needed some moisture.

Landon raised his head when a shadow passed slowly over the fallen man. He smiled crookedly when a circling buzzard flapped its pinions with racous cries of disappointment. Then the vulture winged away through the clear blue, and the desert man returned to his ministrations.

An hour passed while he shaded the wasted bulk with his own big body, and worked his magic until the swollen tongue receded into the oral cavity. Grant Farnol was blistered and beaten by the desert, but his heart was still beating strongly.

Landon took a small drink from the canteen and stretched slowly to his feet. His muscles cracked when he lifted the unconscious man to the saddle and tied Farnol in place.

The sun made no shadow when Landon led his horse from Hell's Basin. Soon they came to the first street marking the boundary of Paradise.

Landon lifted Farnol down and laid him in the shade of a willow. He reached for the canteen and poured a few drops of water between the sagging lips. Then he sat down on his boot heels to watch and wait.

He wondered what would happen if Adam Tyrone and his men came riding into Paradise and found the big gambler helpless.

Farnol stirred slightly when the moisture penetrated the dry membrane of his mouth. He swallowed painfully and opened his eyes when a few drops of water trickled down his parched throat, while Landon waited to judge the measure of a man.

Few would survive the *Jornado de Muerte;* fewer still would preserve their sanity if they did so. Farnol had tasted only a part of Hell's Basin in the heat of the day, but those few hours had robbed him of most of his strength, and forty pounds of flesh.

His dark eyes were red-rimmed and bloodshot when he stared at Joel Landon for a long moment. Neither spoke, but the desert man knew that Farnol's mind was normal. The black beady eyes held steady with a glittering intensity, like the eyes of a snake that seeks to charm its prey.

"It is high noon, Farnol. Get on your feet. We are going to Paradise, you and me!"

Farnol opened his eyes slowly and stared for a long moment. There might be those in Paradise who would change the balance of power. Some of his men might have escaped on horseback, and Farnol would always be a gambler. He'd take a chance.

He nodded slowly and staggered to his feet.

"You walk this time," the deputy said quietly, and swung up to the saddle. "You might get an idea to ride off and leave me on foot." He stared down at Farnol and said slowly: "You will never set another man on foot in the desert!"

Grant Farnol said nothing. He took a deep breath to gather his strength for the ordeal. Farnol's fingers touched the handle of his gun when he took his first step forward. His mind began to race with new plans when he squared his drooping shoulders and started up the sandy road toward the open square. There might come a moment when Joel Landon would be careless.

His legs were heavy, and they trembled with weakness from his long ordeal. Farnol gritted his teeth and plodded along, with Landon staying just out of reach. Both were silent now, busy with their own thoughts. Farnol drew a long deep breath when his swinging hand lightly touched his holstered gun.

A man came out of the General Store and stared with his eyes shaded under his hand, against the glare of the midday sun. For a long moment he watched before running inside to shout the news. Men poured out on the dirt sidewalk and passed the word along until the business street was lined with unbelieving spectators. Here was something they had long hoped for but had given up as impossible.

A thunder of hooves came from the other end of the street and a band of men rode in from the desert.

Grant Farnol stopped suddenly, and turned his big head to listen. His half-closed eyes widened when he recognized old Adam Tyrone at the head of his men. He craned forward for a better look, and then he caught his breath sharply. These were not his men, deputized to carry the law he had made in Paradise!

He turned to study the stern face of Joel Landon. The deputy marshal jerked a thumb toward the store.

"March," he ordered quietly. "There is shade enough in front of the Post Office. You will feel better there, and some of your strength will return to you. Right now you are very weak."

Farnol knew what Landon was doing to him. He set his jaw and continued up the street. The crowd was staring at the oncoming riders in silence. Then the old man who had first spread the alarm spoke in a loud whisper of awe.

"By God! It's the riders of Purgatory with old Adam Tyrone and Tiny Sutton riding in the lead. It looks like Grant Farnol overplayed his hand at last. Look at 'em come!"

Landon reined in at the store and swung down to the ground. Farnol scowled at the men under the broad wooden awning while he found the shade. His big shoulders squared back when eyes began to lower under his gaze, like they always had done when he looked a man full in the face. Joel Landon watched with a little smile pulling at the corners of his hard mouth.

The Purgatory men were dismounting in silence. Tiny Sutton had his left arm in a bandanna sling, and several of the mountain cowboys wore bandages. They watched Landon with a deep respect which was more complete because of their silence.

Old Adam Tyrone stroked his long white beard. He held up a hand for silence when an angry murmur of voices rose behind him. His eyes were watching the face of Grant Farnol, but he spoke to Landon.

"Eve?" and his deep voice was a pleading whisper. "You found her, son?"

"She is safe," Landon answered quietly. "She was sleeping in Farnol's house when I rode out on the desert to meet the boss of Paradise. He was a pitiful sight all alone out there

I watched him crawl on his hands and knees until the desert had whipped him to a frazzle. Now he knows how it feels."

His lips twitched a trifle when he pointed carelessly at his towering prisoner. Farnol and Adam Tyrone were the biggest men in the crowd, and now Farnol was staring at the deputy marshal.

"Eve Tyrone at my house?" he muttered hoarsely. "Who took her there?"

"It does not matter, but Rory O'Hara brought her," Landon answered in the same low tone. "He was the only one of your men to leave the valley alive."

His eyes were watching the big gambler as he spoke. He could read the swift disappointment in the outlaw's dark face when Farnol heard the news of his defeat for the first time. Landon's hands hung loosely at his sides while he waited for what he knew was coming.

The gambler straightened slowly to his full height. His right hand slapped down for the gun on his leg without warning. The heavy weapon cleared leather like a flash of heat lightning, but Joel Landon made no move to defend himself.

Grant Farnol thumbed the hammer back and triggered three times within the space of a heart beat. His big arm jerked grotesquely to meet the kicking buck on the recoil. Men held their breaths while they waited for the explosions which did not materialize.

Tiny Sutton shifted his boots like a dancer. Then he went for his old forty-five Peacemaker, with a soft moan splitting his thin bloodless lips.

Joel Landon stepped swiftly in front of the little gunfighter while his own right hand jerked up to cover Farnol. The gambler's arm was drawing back when he realized that his gun was empty. Flame roared from Landon's fist to kick the empty weapon from the long clutching fingers, just as Farnol attempted to throw the heavy gun.

The gambler moved back a step and stared down at his empty hand. A trickle of blood oozed slowly from a shallow wound on his thumb. Tiny Sutton shouted hoarsely, making no attempt to hide his blazing anger.

"You just pulled his stinger, Joel. Been me, I'd have drilled that big killer dead center, and then stomped him with my boots!"

"But I'm not you, Tiny," Landon said quietly. "I know I haven't been whipped out of the herd as long as you have been, and I had to remember that I'm the law here in Paradise just now."

Farnol lowered his massive head and swayed unsteadily. Adam Tyrone glanced with disapproval at Sutton, and then he turned to face the Paradise crowd.

"The law does not advocate cold killing," he said sternly. "Me and mine have come home again," and now his rich mellow voice held a note of pride. "We are free like the rest of you folks, thanks to Deputy Marshal Joel Landon!"

The tall desert man shrugged with embarrassment when the crowd gave him a ringing cheer. He stepped up to Grant Farnol and waited until the gambler raised his head and stared sullenly. His black eyes were pin-points of hatred while he watched Landon get ready to speak.

"I saved you from the desert, and out there you tried to shoot me and take my horse," Landon accused. "I stayed out of pistol range until your gun ran dry. I knew your belt was empty; knew your gun was the same way just now."

Farnol listened with his head turned partly to the side. Sutton glowered and nudged Landon. "Tell him," he muttered.

"I have a Federal warrant against you for murder, Grant Farnol," Landon said clearly, but with out raising his drawling voice. "Anything you say will be used against you."

"There doesn't seem much to say," Farnol sneered, and his eyes glared at the tall deputy.

Farnol held out his right hand and studied the deep scratch on his thumb. Tiny Sutton advanced like a cat, shedding the years of exile from his wiry frame. A pair of handcuffs clicked around Farnol's thick wrists, and the crowd sighed with relief.

"I feel better about you now, Farnol," Sutton said grimly. "And I'd still use a gun on you if you got brave and went on the prod again!"

Landon frowned and shook his head. He stepped out and faced the crowd, and they waited respectfully for him to speak.

"You need a new sheriff here in Paradise, men," he began slowly. "Have you anyone special in mind?"

The old storekeeper stepped forward and laid a gnarled

hand on Tiny Sutton's shoulder. He faced the crowd expectantly, smiling at what he read in their faces.

"You damn right we've got some one in mind," he shouted. "Tiny Sutton was our sheriff before Farnol came in here with his gang of killers. She's been hell here in Paradise ever since Tiny left. Welcome back home, you Purgatory men, and we'll hold a special election right away. We aim to make Tiny Sutton our legal sheriff!"

The little gunfighter stood perfectly still. Then he coughed loudly and wiped a hand across his staring eyes. His head went back as he squared his lean shoulders, but all he could do was nod his grizzled head.

Grant Farnol sighed and began to sag. He stepped closer to Landon and spoke in a low, subdued voice.

"Are you taking me out to Slag City?" he asked tonelessly.

The deputy marshal nodded. "That's why I came up here," he answered gruffly. "You've had a pretty tough time of it, Farnol. Do you feel up to making the trip so soon?"

"Right away," the gambler answered hoarsely. "I feel as good as I ever did in my life. You won't hear me whine any, but I'd like to change clothes before we leave. You got any objections?"

Landon frowned. He turned to glance down at the torn trousers. The white silk shirt was in tatters, and Farnol would need a hat. Tiny Sutton was talking quietly to the crowd, and the deputy spoke softly to Adam Tyrone.

"See that Tiny gets elected according to the law," he told the old leader. "Farnol wants to change his clothes, and I can't very well refuse him now. I'll bring Eve back with me when I return, but you better stay here with your men."

"I'll go with you," Tyrone offered eagerly, but Landon shook his head and pointed to the crowd.

"Your place is here, Adam," he said quietly. "I'll be back inside half an hour, and then I start to Slag City with my prisoner. You saw me when I finished that walk across Hell's Basin, and Farnol does not feel any better than I did that afternoon."

"I'd face you right now with an even break," the gambler offered viciously.

"You'll face a judge and jury," Landon promised quietly. "Now let's get on up to your house!"

14

THE CROWD WAS SILENT when Landon took Farnol by the arm and walked up the narrow street. They turned at the corner and headed for the old house hidden in the clump of willows. The gambler remained silent, and Landon was thinking of Tiny Sutton.

The election would be only a formality, because the crowd had already indicated their choice. Landon smiled when the noise of the crowd was left behind. The sun was beating down through layers of heat waves. Both men sighed with relief when they reached the shade of the desert willows. Landon stopped to speak to Farnol.

"Don't try any tricks," he warned. "You can get your change of clothes, but I will be right behind you."

"It would be different if you were in front of me," Farnol sneered. "With the difference in my holster."

Landon climbed the steps and pushed the door open with his left hand. He stepped in first to awaken Eve Tyrone. His right hand darted down to his holster when he saw that the couch was empty. Something crashed down on his head before he could turn, and he went to his knees with blinding lights exploding in front of his eyes.

The gun tumbled from his hand and slid across the floor just before Landon slumped to the spur-splintered planking. A man jumped across his prostrate form and collided with' Grant Farnol in the doorway. Boots scuffed on the porch, and then Rory O'Hara whirled with a gun in his big freckled fist.

Landon did not see the girl crouching against the side wall just behind the open door. Eve Tyrone caught up the deputy's sliding gun when O'Hara tried to ear back the hammer of his weapon for a shot. The girl pressed trigger and jerked back when the heavy gun bucked up in her hand. Rory O'Hara spilled sideways from the porch and thumped to the ground.

Eve leaped to her feet and slammed the heavy door when O'Hara came to his knees with a gun in his left hand. She heard the rush of boots toward the back of the house, and then the rattle of hooves as two horses broke into a dead run.

The girl hesitated with the gun hanging in her shaking hand. She knew that her bullet had hit Rory O'Hara, but she was thankful that she had not killed him. She went to her knees when Joel Landon groaned softly. She gathered up his head, cradling it against her swelling breast, and her dark eyes filled with tears when she saw the trickle of crimson seeping down from his thick brown hair.

His eyes were closed, and except for the moaning sound, the deputy marshal seemed like a man asleep.

"Joel," she pleaded softly. "Please wake up, Joel. I knew you would come for me. Something told me that you would come, and you did!"

Landon moaned ánd stirred restlessly. Eve Tyrone sobbed and held him close. His eyes opened slowly and stared at the curly head so close to his own. He tried to sit up, but Eve tightened her arms and sprinkled his face with tears of relief.

The desert man relaxed again and closed his eyes. His head ached from the blow of the heavy gun barrel, and then he remembered his prisoner. New strength flowed through his muscles. He struggled up and glared about the room.

"Farnol!" he rasped hoarsely. "Where is he?"

"He's gone, Joel," the girl told him jerkily. "But you are badly hurt. Rory O'Hara hit you on the head with his gun just as you came through the door. He hit you with his left hand, or the blow might have killed you."

"But Rory O'Hara and Smiley," the dazed man murmured. He lowered his head in an effort to think better. "It looked like him, but he was tied up," he muttered thickly.

Landon tried to get to his feet, but he fell back exhausted. The door burst in suddenly, and Tiny Sutton was on the porch crouching over his drawn gun, with the Purgatory men behind him. He came in when he saw Landon down on the floor, and his voice was a savage growl when he spoke to the staring girl.

"Where's Grant Farnol? Speak up, gal!"

"He escaped," Eve answered quickly. "Rory O'Hara came back here just before Joel arrived with Farnol. O'Hara clubbed Joel over the head with his gun, and Joel lost his own gun before he dropped to his knees. I caught it when it slid across the floor, and I—shot O'Hara!"

"You killed him?" Sutton shouted.

The girl shook her head. "I couldn't," she whispered with a shudder running through her body. "I only wounded him, and then I slammed the door. They ran to the horses and rode away toward the Vermillion Cliffs!"

"You take care of Landon," the sheriff ordered gruffly, and he turned to the Purgatory men. "Get your horses and follow me," he told them. "We'll ride those two down before sunset. Farnol has my cuffs on his wrists, and Rory O'Hara is wounded. They won't get far!"

"Wait, Tiny," Landon said weakly. "You can't stand a ride like that back in the badlands, wounded like you are. If that shoulder of yours starts bleeding again it will give you a lot of trouble."

"It will just remind me how Grant Farnol ought to be bleeding right now," Sutton answered grimly. "I don't aim to quit the trail until either me or Farnol is past all bleeding."

"Look, Sheriff," Landon said quietly, and he took a deep breath to make his voice stronger. "I made you a deputy for the ride here to Paradise. Now your own folks have elected you sheriff again, and that means that you've got to turn back when you get to the county line. Remember that you are a lawman, Sutton."

Sutton whirled swiftly with a scowl twisting his thin face. Paradise County ended at the foot of the Vermillion Cliffs, and it also marked the jurisdiction of the doughty little gunfighter. From there on the trail would have to be followed by Federal officers, and Deputy Marshal Landon was in no condition to ride.

"It's not like you to stick on a point like that, Joel," Sutton said slowly, and then his narrowed eyes lighted with understanding. "You've seen how fast Farnol is with his tools," he accused bitterly. "You're saving him for your own powder smoke!"

Landon slowly nodded his head. He saw Eve Tyrone catch her breath quickly when she turned to him with an expression of terror in her wide brown eyes, while Tiny Sutton accused him of selfishness with his eyes, and said never a word with his lips.

"You can't do that, Joel," the girl whispered. "Your work was finished when you drove Grant Farnol and his gang from Paradise. Rory O'Hara is the only one of Farnol's gang left, and he is wounded twice."

"That's right," Sutton agreed promptly. "Your work is all done here, Landon."

"Looks like it was only started," the tall desert man contradicted, and now he was regaining his strength. "My orders were to bring Farnol in—*dead or alive!*"

Tiny Sutton stared at Landon for a long time while he tried to form a plan. He remembered the men behind him when shifting boots shuffled restlessly on the worn floor behind him. If he could overtake the fleeing outlaws before they reached the badlands, he would be acting within his rights. But time was wasting and adding to the start of the fugitives.

"I'll be seeing you, Landon," he growled shortly, and he ran to his horse and climbed the saddle without a backward glance. "C'mon, you Purgatory men!"

Joel Landon heard Adam Tyrone coming toward the house, and he turned toward the door to avoid the accusing eyes of Eve Tyrone. The events of the night and morning had moved swiftly, and there had been little time for rest, none for sleep. He shrugged his wide shoulders. A man could make up his sleep later.

The room began to whirl dizzily, and Landon caught himself just in time to avoid a fall. He sat down on the couch with his hands groping blindly. The girl was at his side instantly with a little cry of concern. She was supporting him when the old patriarch came through the front door.

"He is badly hurt, Gramps," she explained quickly, before the old man could speak. "Rory O'Hara hit him on the head with his gun. Then Joel argued a long time with Tiny Sutton, and the excitement has been too much for him. Now he needs rest and sleep."

"And food," Tyrone added. "You say he took a blow on the head?"

"When he came to get me," Eve said worriedly.

"And Grant Farnol escaped," Tyrone said quietly. "Tiny Sutton and our Purgatory men rode out after him. I knew it when I saw them heading toward the badlands."

Eve Tyrone tightened her arms about the deputy marshal when he swayed forward. She knew that Joel Landon was conscious, but he was also too weak to ride. A smile curved

99

her full red lips, and she held Landon down without effort when he tried to get to his feet.

Landon shook his head impatiently when the room continued to whirl. He tried to fight back the dizziness that swirled about him like a hazy fog. Objects were beginning to dim before his eyes, and he tried desperately to summon his flagging strength.

"I'll get him," he muttered drowsily. "I'll bring him in if it is the last thing I do!"

"Tiny Sutton will save you the trouble," Tyrone said soothingly. "And he has enough good men with him to do the job."

"It's my work," Landon argued angrily, but now his eyes were closed.

Adam Tyrone changed the subject when he saw Eve shudder violently. He read the deep fear in her brown eyes, and he saw the girl tighten her arms with an instinctive gesture of protection.

"How did Farnol escape?" he asked quietly.

"I was asleep on the couch," the girl explained, and Landon breathed easier and leaned forward as though he were listening. "I felt some one staring down at me," the girl continued in a husky voice. "Rory O'Hara was pointing a gun at me when I opened my eyes."

Landon again tried to gather his legs under him and failed. The girl pulled him down and tightened her arms around his shoulders. Adam Tyrone frowned but remained silent. He was remembering Farnol's threat against Landon at the Post Office.

"It was terrible," Eve whispered. "O'Hara said he would kill me if I made a sound. He boasted that he had killed deputy marshal Smiley who was taking him to prison down at Slag City. He said one more killing wouldn't matter now."

"But how did Rory O'Hara escape from the deputy?" Tyrone asked slowly.

"They stopped to make camp last night, and O'Hara asked for a drink," the girl answered just above her breath. O'Hara kicked Smiley when the deputy held a canteen to O'Hara's lips. Kicked him in the stomach, and in some way he got Smiley's gun and killed him. Then he found the keys to the handcuffs. I feel responsible, Gramps. I could have killed Rory O'Hara and saved all this trouble, but I only wounded him!"

Joel Landon moaned softly and tried to open his eyes. A terrible pain was clamping his head like a steel vise, and threatening to rob him of consciousness. He drew a long deep breath and fought to control the recurring waves of dizziness.

Adam Tyrone was stroking his long white beard thoughtfully, trying to find some solution. His face was sad as he watched Landon, wanting to do something to help the man who had helped his people so much.

Landon sighed and slumped forward. Eve motioned the old man away when he came forward to help. She cradled the unconscious man's head on her shoulder and spoke jerkily.

"That blow might have fractured his skull," she whispered. "Rory O'Hara hit him so hard with the gun that the blow broke the scalp even under Joel's heavy hat. He is unconscious now, Gramps. We've got to take him back to Purgatory. He might be ill for a long time."

"He can rest back there in the quiet hills," Tyrone agreed, and he tried to make his voice sound confident. "We owe him more than we can ever repay, but at least we can try to even the score. His first thought was of you after we rode into Paradise."

"I know," the girl whispered. "He came through the door first to warn me, before allowing Farnol to enter. If he had only pushed Grant Farnol in first!"

"Joel Landon never thought first of himself," Tyrone said slowly. He turned his head to listen. "I wonder who is coming?" he said with a frown.

Footsteps hurried up the stairs, and Tyrone sighed with relief and holstered his six-shooter when Doctor Telford came through the door. Telford stopped and stared at the slumping man in Eve Tyrone's arms. Then he went to the couch and dropped to his knees in front of the pair.

"Tell me quick!" he barked. "Is he hurt very bad? Where is he wounded?"

"His head," the girl answered, with a catch in her husky voice. "He was struck over the head with a gun. He regained consciousness and was talking to us, and then he lost consciousness again while Gramps and I were trying to decide what to do."

The doctor felt for a pulse and shook his head slowly. His long slender fingers moved gently across the deep scalp

101

wound, exploring carefully. Old Adam watched in silence until the doctor turned to him and spoke in a low voice.

"You better get a wagon, Mayor. I don't believe that his skull is fractured, but I cannot be sure. I do know that he is suffering from a severe concussion, and it could be fatal unless we act at once. He might be out of his head for several days. We had better take him where we can watch him every minute until he has entirely recovered. He will not know what he is doing, but his sub-conscious mind might drive him to do what he thinks is his duty."

"You mean he might wake up and want to start after Grant Farnol," Tyrone said slowly. "You are telling me that his strength will come back before he recovers entirely from shock."

"That is exactly what I mean," Telford answered quietly. "I can give him something to keep him quiet during the ride back to Purgatory. You have a large and comfortable house there, and there will be no excitement like there will be here in town."

"I'll go right away, doctor," Tyrone agreed, and he left the room. He put on his hat and hurried toward the livery stable at the edge of town.

Telford watched the injured man with an expression of deep concern on his bearded face. Then he turned and studied the face of the girl.

"Better let him lie flat," he suggested and waited until she laid Landon on the low couch. "I will need help with this case," he continued sternly. "Can I depend on you this time, Eve Tyrone?"

The girl caught her breath when she remembered Baldy Sanger and the time she had failed because of her lack of faith in Joel Landon. Her brown eyes filled with unshed tears when she nodded her head.

"I will do anything you say, Doctor Telford," she promised earnestly. "Do you really think he will be out of his head for several days?"

"I am not sure," Telford answered impatiently. "It might cause a temporary loss of memory," he explained more quietly. "I have seen the same thing happen before, especially when the patient had been under a severe mental strain. Landon had his campaign mapped out before the fight last night, and you know what happened. Tiny Sutton was his closest friend here, and Sutton was wounded."

"That was my fault," the girl murmured, with her eyes downcast.

"Yes," Telford agreed. "Then you became hysterical. Sutton and Landon had to forget the fight and take care of you. He rode all night to rescue you, and now ..."

He paused for a moment to let the meaning of his words sink in. Eve Tyrone shuddered, and then she stroked the unconscious man's tousled hair gently, refusing to meet the doctor's stern eyes.

"One of us will have to be with him all the time," Telford went on. "He rode through the desert all night, worrying about you. He had heard what Farnol had said about you, and that was one of the reasons why he went to find Farnol while he allowed you to sleep. He must have relived his own terrible trip across Hell's Basin, and I know that he meant to let Farnol die."

"But he didn't," Eve said quickly.

"He should have," Telford grunted. "I can see it now. Landon is a desert man; he knew just what to do. He saved Grant Farnol's life, ministered to him, and protected him from the mob. Our boys would have hung Farnol, and saved the state money. But Landon is a lawman first, and he did his duty. Now we must do ours."

"But he will recover," Eve whispered. "We will give him every care until he is entirely his old self again."

"You knew him well when he was his old self," Telford warned. "And like every woman since the original Eve, you tried to change him, and make him into something else."

"I thought he was a killer," the girl whispered. "The look in his eyes last night!"

"He is a killer," Telford said sternly. "Farnol meant to kill every man in Purgatory. Can't you remember that fact?"

"Don't talk that way to me!" Eve Tyrone said angrily.

Telford faced her with blazing eyes. "I don't know that I want your help on this case," he said coldly. "You think more of yourself and your foolish pride than you do of those who were willing to die that you might live!"

Eve Tyrone stared, and then her eyes dropped. "I'm sorry, doctor," she murmured. "Anything you say. I'll do anything!"

"That's better, if I could be sure," the doctor said quietly. "A doctor's first duty is to his patient; others do not matter.

Landon is much that way, too. His first duty is to his oath of office."

"It might be better if he did not remember," she said in a whisper. "It might save his life if he forgot."

The doctor turned and studied her face with a trace of anger in his glance. Then he set his lips in a straight line as he slowly shook his head.

"Joel Landon is a law officer," he said sternly. "He has his work to do, just as I now have mine. It is the most important thing in his life, and Landon is a man of character. It took years to build that kind of a character, and it must not be changed!"

"He is fine and honest," Eve whispered. "Sometimes he is like two different people. I like the other one best. The man he is when he is *not* a law officer."

Joel Landon stirred and sighed deeply. Fine beads of moisture stood out on his forehead, and the girl took her handkerchief and wiped his brow.

"We won't tell him," she said stubbornly. "His orders were to bring Grant Farnol in—dead or alive. If he forgets about Farnol, Joel Landon will live!"

Doctor Telford caught his breath with a sharp intake. He leaned forward to stare into the girl's narrowed eyes.

"You would do that to him, after what he has done for the people of Purgatory?" he asked. "You would put yourself before his honor and his duty, before all the things he has spent his life to build?"

"I would put his life before all these things," the girl answered firmly. "I would do it because we owe him more than we can ever hope to repay. Grant Farnol would kill him if they ever met, but nothing could stop Joel from trying to do his duty—if he remembered his orders!"

"I could stop him until he was strong enough to resume his duties. He will recover in a few days with proper rest and care."

The rattle of wheels stopped whatever reply the girl might have made. Adam Tyrone and the driver came into the room, and Telford gave them instructions for moving Landon.

They carried him down the steps and laid him gently on a bedspring in the bed of the wagon. Eve sat behind and held Landon's hand. Adam climbed to the driver's seat and picked up the reins.

"Climb in, Doctor Telford," he whispered.

"No need to whisper, he won't awaken," Telford told him. "Let's start back home, old friend."

"So much has happened in such a short time," Tyrone said wearily. "I am not proud of some of my actions and neither is Eve. We will not make the same mistakes again."

"Amen," Telford said heartily. "I sincerely hope you are right."

He glanced back at the girl but she avoided meeting his eyes. Adam Tyrone started the horses across the cactus-studded sand toward the row of tombstones.

Dawn was lighting up the sky when Tyrone stopped the team in front of his own house.

The sleeping man stirred restlessly. Telford felt for a pulse and counted on his watch. The heartbeat was strong and steady; physical recovery would be swift and certain. But mentally?

The sleeping man moved slowly, and then opened his eyes. For a brief moment he stared at the doctor. He nodded carelessly and felt his head with his left hand. Little veins stood out on his forehead with the effort he was making to remember.

"Howdy, Doc," he said quietly, "Farnol hit me hard back there in the sheriff's office. Things went black for a time."

Telford frowned and gripped the wounded man's right hand. He leaned forward to concentrate with all the force of his will. His voice was slow and concise when he spoke.

"Think hard," he suggested. "It was Rory O'Hara who hit you, Joel. And it happened in Grant Farnol's house over in Paradise!"

The gray eyes narrowed slightly, and Landon slowly shook his head. "You're wrong about that, Doc," he muttered. "I was talking to Joe Bodie, and he got careless. I took his gun away from him. Then Farnol slapped me to sleep with the barrel of his gun. I remember the whole thing now."

"We will carry him to the room he used when he first came to us," Tyrone said softly.

Doctor Telford climbed from the wagon and stretched his cramped muscles. "Landon gave me back my manhood," the slender doctor said. "I might repay him in part if I can give him back his memory."

Eve Tyrone said not a word. She knew what Joel Landon would do if he remembered. She helped carry the sleeping man to the back room.

IT WAS NOON when Landon yawned lazily and opened his eyes.

For a moment he stared at the pretty face leaning above him. He became conscious of a pressure on his fingers. He smiled and gently withdrew his right hand.

"I remember you," he said slowly. "You are Eve."

"And you are Joel Landon, a desert man," the girl said pleasantly. "You were looking for the lost Indian gold mine, remember? I will help you find it back in the hills."

Landon's face changed, and a frown appeared between his eyes. He stared blankly at the ceiling, and then he slowly stroked his chin. His head turned slightly to look at the girl.

"Later," he said quietly. "But first there is something else that I must do. Something very important. If I could only remember what it was."

Eve Tyrone watched his face anxiously, and for a moment she forgot to breathe. If he remembered about the fight in Farnol's house back in Paradise . . . ?

"You must get well and strong first," she told him gently. "It was a long walk across the desert, and you had no food or water. You have been here for quite awhile, but you are nearly well now."

"Where's Doc?" Landon asked suddenly. "He was here with me, and I remember him saying something about me walking across the desert. It seems to me that I always ride a horse." He studied her face. "Doc mentioned something about Tiny Sutton," he said slowly. "Then I must have gone to sleep again."

"You are a desert man," the girl answered with a smile. "You have seen what the desert can do to a man. But you made it across safely, and you were looking for the lost gold mine. Don't you remember now?"

Landon wrinkled his brow and stared at the ceiling. Then he sighed deeply and returned his glance to the girl.

"I remember now," he said softly. "Grant Farnol came up behind me and hit me over the head with his gun. I was in the sheriff's office, and they led me out to the end of the street when I aroused. They took my horse, and set me afoot. I walked across Hell's Basin. Seemed like I never would make it toward the end, but I reckon I did, or I wouldn't be here."

"You made it, but you were very weak," the girl assured him gently. "Now all you have to do is rest until you get strong again."

"My head hurts," Landon murmured, and he closed his eyes.

"You must be hungry," the girl said with a smile. "I will call Martha, and have her bring you some warm food. You will soon be well and strong again, and then we can look for the lost mine."

Landon looked at her, sighed deeply, and slowly nodded. Several times he raised his hand to stroke his head, and the girl watched him intently. He opened his eyes again when Martha came in with a tray, and Eve propped him up with pillows and helped him with the food.

"Good," he said slowly. "I am hungry as a bear."

"You were as sleepy as one, too," Eve said. "But you slept well, and that is a good sign."

Landon was finishing the food on the tray when Doctor Telford came into the room. He stopped abruptly when he saw that Landon was awake. His keen eyes darted to the face of Eve Tyrone, and studied her features for a long moment.

"Did you help him?" he asked sharply.

"Yes," the girl answered without hesitation. "He remembers walking across Hell's Basin. He also remembers that he was looking for the lost gold mine."

Telford stared at her and set his thin lips.

"Think hard, Joel Landon," he commanded sternly. "What was the last thing you remember?"

Landon turned and studied the doctor's face. "Grant Farnol hit me with his gun," he answered slowly. "I was in the sheriff's office with Joe Bodie at the time. Then I walked across the desert."

"That was a long time ago," Telford said sternly. "Now think hard. You had a fight," he reminded. "Rory O'Hara was hiding behind a door and he hit you with a gun!"

"Grant Farnol hit me," Landon corrected carelessly, and he closed his eyes. "Now I've got to find that lost Indian gold mine."

The doctor turned and stared at Eve Tyrone. Then he got

up abruptly and left the room, nodding for the girl to follow him to the hall. He gripped her shoulders with both hands.

"You didn't want him to remember," he accused.

The girl met his blazing eyes without wavering. "Yes," she admitted honestly. "If he started after Grant Farnol now, Joel Landon would surely be killed. He does not even remember what Farnol looks like, and he is still very weak. I reminded him first about the lost gold mine. I did it deliberately."

The doctor stared for a moment, and then his eyes somehow lost their hardness. He nodded his head as though he had suddenly found the answer.

"You love him," he accused softly. "You do not want to lose him now."

The girl glared at him with her head held high. Then she nodded and lowered her eyes to hide the scalding tears. Telford frowned for a time, then cupped his hand under her chin and slowly raised her head.

"It might be for the best," he admitted quietly. "But when Joel Landon is well and strong again, Eve Tyrone—what then?"

The girl caught his hands as a look of terror widened her eyes. For a moment she could not speak. Then the words rushed from her lips like a torrent.

"You must not tell him!" she cried. "He has some right to happiness!"

"Look at me, Eve," the doctor commanded sternly. "Landon will remember some day, when he recovers from the shock. He will despise you for what you have done to him now. Is that the way to give him happiness? Think hard about that time when he will surely remember."

"He won't," the girl whispered desperately. "I am going to help him find the lost Indian gold mine back in the hills. It might take a long time!"

"Go back to him now," the doctor said wearily. "But remember well what I have told you. Think of my words when you are trying to keep him from remembering. No one can hurt you as much as you can hurt yourself. Remember well, Eve."

A boot scraped on the floor. Joel Landon came out into the hall fully dressed.

"My gun," he said quietly. "I couldn't find it, and I don't feel fully dressed. I won't, until I have it again."

Telford smiled and walked back into the bedroom. He

108

went to a bureau and opened a top drawer. Landon had followed him wonderingly. Telford reached in and picked up a shell-studded belt which he handed to Landon. He watched the deputy marshal's face closely to observe his reactions.

Landon buckled the belt around his lean hips and fastened the tie-backs low from force of habit. Now the holster would not flap when he mounted a horse, or go up with the gun if he made a speedy draw. He slipped the heavy gun a time or two to fit it to the moulded holster. Then he raised his head and smiled as though satisfied.

"Now I feel like I have all my clothes on," he said with a chuckle. "I just remembered something, and I want to have a talk with Tiny Sutton."

"Tiny has not returned yet," Telford answered quickly. "He's looking for a man."

"Tiny won't have to worry about Farnol any more," Landon said confidently. "I sent him to Siag City with Deputy Marshal Smiley."

"Smiley is dead!" Telford said sharply.

"You mean Shawn O'Hara is dead," Eve corrected quickly, and she turned to Landon. "We won't start looking for the lost mine until tomorrow," she told him with a warm smile.

"The mine can wait," Telford said stubbornly. He walked up to stand squarely in front of Landon. "Rory O'Hara killed Deputy Smiley and escaped," he said slowly, and carefully spaced each word for emphasis. "It was O'Hara who hit you over the head with his gun!"

"O'Hara is dead," Landon said impatiently. "And I saw Tiny Sutton put the handcuffs on Grant Farnol."

Telford stared, and then made a mental recapitulation. He knew that Landon was confused about the two O'Haras, just as he was about being struck on the head on two different occasions. The injured man could not separate the incidents in his clouded mind. Doctor Telford set his lips tightly. He sighed gently to acknowledge defeat. Joel Landon was smiling at the girl. The doctor stepped aside when Eve led Landon from the room. He followed them down to the long porch where Adam Tyrone was seated in a big easy chair.

"Howdy, Joel," the old Mayor greeted warmly, and he arose to grip the deputy marshal's extended hand. "I've been waiting to thank you for what you have done for the people of Purgatory."

"Forget it," the desert man answered with a smile.

"We won't ever forget it," Adam said. "You will stay here with us before you continue your search?"

"I reckon I will," Landon answered with a nod. "I've heard that the lost Indian mine is back there somewhere in Eden Valley, but we won't start looking for it until to-morrow."

"Mine?" the old man repeated, and he turned to stare at his granddaughter. "What about that old mine?"

"He came back here to look for the lost Indian mine," Eve Tyrone said quickly, before Landon could answer. "I promised to help him search for it, and it will occupy his mind while he is regaining his strength."

"But it won't help his memory any," Telford interrupted harshly.

Adam Tyrone glanced up and then set his jaw stubbornly. He knew that there had been a clash of wills between the doctor and the girl, and his heavy eyebrows drew together when he saw the girl smile triumphantly.

"What about Grant Farnol?" Tyrone demanded.

Landon smiled carelessly. "I caught Farnol," he answered lightly. "He won't trouble you any more."

Tyrone caught his breath and turned to stare at Doctor Telford. The doctor turned his back on Landon and jerked his head toward the girl. Eve squared her shoulders and faced the old man defiantly.

"It will take Joel some time to get over the shock he received," she said meaningfully. "I am sure that it will help him just to get back in the hills for a few days."

"Now see here, Eve," the old leader began harshly. "What does Doctor Telford think about all this talk about hunting for a lost gold mine?"

"He thinks it will do Joel a world of good," the girl answered steadily. "Don't you, Doctor Telford?"

"Under certain conditions, it might be just the thing he needs," Telford answered quietly, but his eyes were watching the girl. "The three of us will ride back there tomorrow. I can look after my patient, and act as chaperone at the same time."

Eve Tyrone stared at him with her brown eyes flashing. The doctor returned her gaze without winking, and his features were adamant. The girl finally lowered her eyes and bowed her head.

"We will all ride back together," she agreed, and turned to the old man. "Did the men get back from Paradise yet?" she asked, as they turned again to Landon.

"I didn't hear them ride in, and I'm worried about Tiny Sutton," Tyrone answered, as he accepted the change of subject. "That wound might give him trouble back there in the badlands."

"I'd like to change the bandages," Telford murmured, tugging at his beard to show his worry.

"You can't kill an old hand like Tiny Sutton," Landon said with a quiet chuckle. "When are you expecting him back?"

"Some time tonight, unless they have trouble," Tyrone answered, and it was evident that he too was worried. "You and Tiny were the leaders of our fighting men," he continued. "With you back here, and Tiny wounded, the men might take things into their own hands."

"What things?" Landon asked with a puzzled gleam in his gray eyes. "I thought we had everything cleaned up."

"You did," Eve answered quickly, and she looped her fingers about the deputy's left arm. "Let's walk down to the stables, Joel," she suggested. "We will have to take a packhorse with us back to Eden Valley, and we can look over the riding stock."

"Might be a good idea," Landon agreed, and they walked away from the big house.

Adam Tyrone waited until the two were out of sight. Then he turned to Telford and motioned to a chair with his left hand. The doctor sat down and waited for the old leader to speak.

"What's all this talk about the lost gold mine?" Tyrone demanded. "Landon meant to hunt for Grant Farnol, and not that old mine!"

"Landon had a chance to remember," the doctor said slowly, after a long pause. "If he had been reminded of what had happened just as soon as his mind was clear enough to grasp the details, he would have picked up the train of events in their proper order. He does not remember that Grant Farnol escaped. All he remembers is that Farnol hit him with a gun in Joe Bodie's office, and that was before he was sentenced to death. He remembers walking across Hell's Basin. He knows people, but he has forgotten events."

"But he remembers that he captured Farnol," Tyrone said with a frown.

"Eve was with him when he awoke," Telford answered reluctantly. "She told him that he was searching for a lost Indian mine. That was the first thing he heard, and his mind seized upon it as an objective. Now he thinks that is the reason he is back here."

"My granddaughter did that to him?" the old man whispered in a stricken voice. "She did that, after all he has suffered for us?"

The doctor said with stern determination, "Eve can take the lead up to a certain point, but after all, I am a medical man, and I owe more than my life to Joel Landon!"

"You mean that you have cured yourself of the curse of strong drink?" Tyrone asked, a gentle smile lighting his face.

"Entirely," the doctor answered. "When the time is right, I will tell Landon all the things he should know for his own protection."

"But if he stays here, he will not need protection," Tyrone said with a puzzled frown. "There will be nothing for him to guard against."

"When he knows all the facts, he won't stay back here," Telford answered, and now his voice was harsh. "He came back here, a Federal officer, to get Grant Farnol, and he will get him."

"You will tell him," Adam Tyrone said gravely, "and Joel Landon will do his duty."

16

THE EARLY MORNING sun was slanting down from the high hills in the east when Landon came into the large kitchen for breakfast. Doctor Telford was talking with Adam Tyrone in the living room, and both men greeted Landon as though nothing had happened. Eve was bringing in hot plates of steaming food. Landon smiled at the girl when he saw that she was dressed for a long ride.

"How are you this morning, Joel?" she asked him.

"I feel fine," he told her. "I can hardly wait until we start back for the hills."

"You will love it back in Eden," she said confidently. "We will start right after breakfast."

Nothing was said about Tiny Sutton and the riders of Purgatory during the meal. The sheriff had not returned, and the girl shook her head and frowned at Doctor Telford when he started to speak. She knew that he was going to mention Sutton, and she changed the subject while her dark eyes watched Telford's scowling face.

"I've always wanted to look for that Indian mine," she began. "It will be just like a holiday after all the hard work we have done."

"What hard work?" Telford asked stubbornly.

"The hard work we have just finished," Eve answered tartly. "Some of us worked harder than others."

She stayed close to Landon when the deputy marshal finished his breakfast and went out for a look at the horses. Adam Tyrone shook hands with Landon, and the deputy climbed his saddle and waited impatiently for Eve and Telford to mount their horses.

"We will be rich when we come back, Gramps," the girl told Tyrone with a smile. "I feel sure we will find the old mine."

"If Joel finds what he looking for, I shall be content," the old man answered gravely. "You know what I mean, Eve," he added, just loud enough for the girl to hear.

"Perhaps we are not of the same mind about what he is looking for," the girl answered bluntly, and a spot of color burned on her high cheeks.

The doctor wisely fell back to lead the pack horse. Eve Tyrone rode up front rubbing stirrups with the deputy, talking with an animation that spoke plainly of the relief she felt, while she led the way toward the foothills. She pointed out landmarks that were as familiar to her as her own back yard. Landon nodded and fixed these marks firmly in his mind.

Big rangy steers branded with the Diamond T were grazing contentedly on the high blue-stem that covered the valley floor. Landon rode along without making any comment for several miles. Then he turned suddenly to the girl with a startled gleam in his gray eyes.

"Shawn O'Hara and his men were to get the cattle," he

113

said harshly. "Grant Farnol wanted both valleys, and the gold!"

"That old gold mine has never been found by white men," she said softly. "We have heard the Indian legends time after time, and I have seen some of the nuggets which came from it. I thought perhaps you would want to see some of them."

"You have some with you?" Landon asked eagerly.

The girl's hand went to her throat and drew a necklace from under her woolen shirt which was open at the neck. She stopped her horse, and Landon urged his horse close and took the necklace in his left hand. His nostrils began to flare when his fingers touched the rough virgin nuggets of gold. Eve Tyrone sighed happily when she realized that he had again forgotten Tiny Sutton and the big gambler.

"Where did you get these?" Landon asked under his breath, but his hand trembled with excitement.

"From a very old Indian," the girl answered. "He gave them to my grandfather before I was born. All I know about it is that the mine was said to be back here somewhere in Eden Valley. Many men have searched for it, but none have been lucky."

"These nuggets came from a pocket," Landon murmured softly. "Do you know of an old stream bed running down from the higher hills?"

Doctor Telford was listening with his head craned forward. His ruddy face took on a new expression when he edged his horse up and interrupted the girl before she could answer.

"There's the dry bed of an old stream up there in that second level of hills," he told Landon, and pointed to a distant rise over toward the east. "There's a cabin there, too. I've been back there several times, when I wanted to be alone."

The doctor's face changed, and his voice was gruff with remembrance. He had found the old river bed and the cabin on a trip he had made to satisfy his craving for drink—away from the reproachful eyes of Adam Tyrone, and the men of Purgatory.

Landon followed Telford's pointing finger to where the hills climbed in a series of steps. For a long moment he studied the formations. Then he motioned with his head for Telford to take the lead.

"Eve and I will follow you, Doc," he said eagerly. "Lead us up there to that old stream bed."

"We will make camp here," the doctor said. "Eve can prepare us something to eat, and you can have a look at that old river bed later."

Landon dismounted and turned his horse into a pole corral. He threw off the ropes that held the pack of provisions on the horse Telford had led, and the two men carried the food inside the cabin.

Telford and Landon sat outside in the shade while Eve busied herself with preparations for a hot meal. The doctor filled an old briar pipe, then turned to Landon with a questioning look in his eyes.

"If you find that old mine?" he asked quietly. "What then, Joel?"

"We haven't found it yet," he answered with a smile, but his hands trembled slightly as he rolled a corn-husk cigarette. "It would make a lot of difference to old Adam Tyrone," he added slowly. "It would give him the money he needs to develop the two valleys."

"Old Adam does not want money," the doctor stated bluntly. "All he wants is to see Eve settled before he takes the long trail into the great Unknown. He has lived most of his life, and before this trouble came to him, he found that life good. He will be thinking mostly of Eve."

Landon shifted uncomfortably and turned to watch the girl in the cabin.

Eve was humming quietly as she rattled the pans on the old wood stove. Landon sighed and tried to turn his eyes away from her lovely face. Eve Tyrone was smiling with a light in her eyes that changed her entire expression, as if she enjoyed some secret thought of her own and was not sharing it with anyone. She was cooking for the first man who had ever caused her to practice deceit.

Doctor Telford watched her work, and then glanced at Landon. He smiled knowingly, and not without a grudging approval. In a way the girl was only partly right in her estimate of his abilities. He shared her secret with her, even if she did not want to admit it.

"Come and get it," she called out cheerily. "Before I throw it in the fire!"

Cow country talk, that. And like hungry men who spend long hours in the saddle, Landon and Telford spoke but little while they ate the thick steaks from a freshly-killed vealer. Landon pushed back his stave chair as soon as the meal was finished. Eve was at his side when he almost ran out to the pole corral to gear the horses.

"We might find something before dark," he murmured, and he tried to keep his voice casual as he tightened his cinches. "The formations look promising from here."

"There's lots of time," Telford reminded him quietly, and he smiled at the girl when he saw her frowning at him. "That old mine has waited quite awhile, according to the legends."

The doctor mounted his horse and led the way through the brush without further comment. He was heading toward a second rise that sloped gently upward. He reined in an hour later, and all three swung to the ground and tied their horses in the saddle of a piñon tree. Landon studied the terrain with interest, waiting for Telford to tell his plan.

"The old river bed is just over that little hill," Telford said carelessly. "I'll stay with the horses while you and Eve take a look. I've been here many a time, and I wouldn't know a gold mine if I stumbled into one."

Landon took a small hammer and a short-handled shovel from behind his cantle. He was like a small boy when he ran up the slope and started down into a little draw where an ancient stream had cut a passage through the rocks. Eve Tyrone was right behind him when he paused in the dry river bed. Then the deputy started up the dry wash like a hound on a hot scent. He seemed to know what he was looking for, and the girl watched with interest.

Landon did not speak for an hour, during which he chipped at rocks here and there, and turned beds of coarse gravel. A hoarse cry burst from his throat when he went to his knees behind a clump of boulders. Dirt began to fly when he started digging with the short shovel. He picked up a small pebble and raised it to his mouth.

The girl watched while his teeth bit the particle. Landon turned swiftly and reached for the necklace around her throat. His fingers touched her soft warm skin, and the girl flushed and lowered her eyes. She gasped when strong arms seized her in a bear-like hug, and the breath grunted from her lungs when Landon forgot his strength and tightened his hold in his exuberance.

"Gold!" he croaked hoarsely. "This old bed is full of pockets, and the pockets are filled with gold nuggets!"

Eve Tyrone was not thinking about the gold. His arms were

around her supple body, crushing her to his powerful chest. The deputy stiffened suddenly when he became conscious of her nearness. Rich color stained his tanned face when he dropped his arms and lowered his head.

"I'm sorry, Eve," he murmured contritely. "I must have been out of my mind."

"No," the girl contradicted softly. "I think you have found your right mind for the first time since you came to Purgatory. And you forget that this is the Valley of Eden."

Landon raised his head quickly and studied her face. Eve was smiling wistfully, and she took one of his hands and pressed it to her cheek.

Landon's arms went around the girl and drew her close, while he looked deep into her brown eyes. Eve smiled and tightened her hands against the flat muscles of his broad back. He lowered his head slowly, watching her flushed face.

"I love you, Eve Tyrone," he said simply, but his deep voice vibrated like the muted tones of a distant bell. "Can I stay here in Eden, and prove myself to you and to old Adam?"

"Joel," the girl whispered with a little catch in her husky voice. "I was afraid you would go away. We want you to stay for always!"

Landon opened his lips a trifle and studied her face for a long time. The laugh wrinkles gathered about her eyes, and Landon found his answer.

"Nothing could take me away from you now," he said earnestly. "I have been searching for something all my life, and now I know that I was looking for you."

His lips moved very slowly, and then he kissed her for the first time. Eve Tyrone closed her eyes and clung to him. Two tall strong bodies moulded to each other until the beats of their hearts blended and throbbed against their eardrums. Landon raised his head and listened intently with a curious expression on his face.

"It sounds like hoofbeats," he murmured softly. "But it was only my heart saying the things I would like to say to you. I feel them, but I can't express that feeling in words."

"Landon!" a hoarse voice shouted. "Where are you, Deputy?"

Landon was jerked back to reality when he recognized the deep gruff voice of Tiny Sutton. He whirled away from Eve, with his right hand dropping to his forgotten six-shooter. Then he was running to meet the little sheriff, who was flinging himself from his sweating horse.

The little gunfighter was thin and worn from exhaustion, and the bandage that held his wounded arm was stained with crimson alkali. He gripped the deputy's hand hard, while a torrent of words rushed from his twisting lips.

"He got away, Joel," Sutton panted. "We had Grant Farnol and Rory O'Hara up on a shelf, and they put up a fight. Rory O'Hara is dead, but Farnol made his escape and got away across the county line. I wanted to take after him, but I remembered my promise to you. I reckon it's up to you now!"

Landon flung the nugget to the ground as a swift change swept over him. His nostrils began to flare, while his gray eyes narrowed at the corners and took on a peculiar smoky color. Eve Tyrone watched him for a moment and then caught desperately at his right hand.

"You can't do it, Joel," she cried. "You promised me that nothing could ever make you leave me now. Don't you re-member, Joel?"

"He's the Federal law, Eve," Sutton said sternly. "Neither Paradise or Purgatory will be safe as long as Grant Farnol is on the loose. Looks to me like you forgot all about your duty, Deputy Marshal Landon!"

Joel Landon growled in his throat as he rubbed the handle of his gun. He had forgotten the girl and his trip to find the lost gold mine. Once more he was picking up the threads of memory, and the fight in Farnol's house came back to him with stunning force.

He had been taking Grant Farnol to his house for a change of clothes and had stepped through the front door first to awaken Eve Tyrone who had been sleeping on the couch. Something had bludgeoned down on his head wth stunning force, and he remembered seeing Rory O'Hara with a heavy gun in his hand. His own weapon had jumped from his nerveless hand, and the girl had caught it up to chop a shot at O'Hara.

Sutton watched in fascination as Landon picked up the the forgotten facts. Landon was leaning forward, straining to recapture every incident. The red giant had fallen from the little porch, and then the heavy door had slammed. After that things had become hazy, but the thud of hooves had told him that the two outlaws were escaping to the badlands. Tiny Sutton had furnished the link between the past and the present.

"Where did you quit the trail?" he demanded of Sutton.

"Right at the edge of the Vermillion Cliffs," the little sheriff answered promptly. "Farnol yelled back that you didn't pack the sand to cut his sign again, and then he was gone!"

"I'll cut his sign, and ride it until I finish what I came here to do," Landon said quietly, and then he gave a little jerk.

He glanced at Eve Tyrone with a little frown of bewilderment clouding his eyes. She averted her face, and Landon squared his shoulders. His right hand slipped the heavy six-shooter in his holster, and his lean jaw thrust out to change the entire expression of his face. Once again he was the fighting man, carrying the law. He looked at Sutton and spoke softly.

"Ride back and wait for me at the cabin, Tiny. I'll be down shortly, but now I want to talk to Eve."

Eve Tyrone turned her back when Tiny Sutton mounted his big horse and rode back over the rise. Joel Landon went to her and put his big hands on her shoulders. He turned her gently, and the girl hid her face against the rough wool of his shirt. For a moment the deputy did not speak. He could feel the warmth of her body, and the excited beat of her heart. Landon moistened his lips when the perfume from her hair filled his nostrils.

"I'll be back, Eve," he began huskily. "But I've got to go now and do my sworn duty. You know that, Eve. I took an oath on the Bible, and I've got to get Grant Farnol!"

"I am not afraid now, Joel," she said and studied his face gravely. "Will you do something for me?" she asked.

"You wouldn't ask it if I couldn't promise like a man," Landon answered earnestly. "Count it already done, Eve."

The girl's hand went to her throat and removed the necklace of nuggets. She raised up on her toes and put it around his neck, and Landon stood quiet while she arranged it under his heavy rough shirt.

"Wear the necklace for me," she whispered. "It will give you good luck. You came back here partly to find the lost Indian mine, and you have found it."

His arms closed about the girl and held her tightly. A swift kiss, and then he was gone from the sandy bank of the old stream. Memory had returned to remind him of his sworn

duty, and deputy marshal Joel Landon was riding to fulfill
that duty when Eve Tyrone rode slowly back to the cabin.

17

DEPUTY MARSHAL JOEL LANDON rode across Hell's
Basin with the moon at his back. It was almost dawn when he
stopped at the livery stable in Paradise to change to a fresh
horse. The sun was rising when he pressed on toward the
brilliant Vermillion Cliffs, and he was deep in the badlands when he stopped at noon for a sandwich of coarse
bread and cold meat.

The way had been long, but something more than physical
strength made the going seem easier—thoughts of Eve Tyrone back in Eden Valley, and old Adam in Purgatory. His
face hardened when he thought of Deputy Smiley. Sutton's
men had buried the murdered officer, and the man who had
killed him. Only Grant Farnol was left of the vicious gang,
but Farnol could gather other recruits about him.

A horse neighed softly from some hiding place deep in
the brush, and the deputy was on his feet like a flash. Five
minutes later he found the animal, lamed in one foot, and
with saddle-sores on its back. The deep imprints of shod
hoofs were plain in the trampled dirt, leading back toward
Paradise.

Landon studied the sign and tightened his lips. A pair of
big boots had made imprints all about, with no attempt to
conceal the plain trail they provided. They were deep to
show that their owner was a heavy man who had stopped
to change horses. Landon made his way back to his own horse
and mounted in grim silence.

He remembered that taunt Grant Farnol had shouted over
his shoulder to Tiny Sutton. Did the gambler really believe
that he, Joel Landon, lacked the courage to bring the law
to him? Was Farnol that sure of his own superiority? The
deputy marshal clicked his teeth and turned his horse to re-
trace his own steps.

The heat was intense in the badlands as Landon rode back
toward Paradise. Now he knew some of the short-cuts, and he
refreshed both the horse and himself at a water-hole he had

marked in his mind on the way north. Then he started on the plain trail again, and the long afternoon passed with the miles as Landon held the horse to a walk.

The sun was sinking when he reached the edge of Paradise and stared at the clump of desert willows where Farnol's house was hidden. Landon rode to the edge of the cover and tied up his horse. He slipped the heavy gun in his holster to make sure against hang, and started for the back of the house, placing each boot down carefully to avoid crackling twigs which might betray his presence.

A deep-chested Morgan horse was tied in the brush near the kitchen door. Landon shucked his spurs when he remembered the first time he had raided Farnol's house. Was the gambler so sure of himself that he did not even think it necessary to maintain a watch?

Landon shrugged and moved closer. He could hear Farnol moving about in the big front room, emptying boxes and opening drawers. The deputy drew a deep breath and started through the kitchen. He reached the front room without making a sound to betray his presence, but a board creaked under his boot just as he stepped into the room.

Grant Farnol whirled like a cat despite his bulk. His hand darted toward the gun on his right leg. He stopped the move when he saw Landon facing him with hand just above his holster. The two men locked glances while the clock on the mantel ticked away a full minute. Farnol was the first to break the long silence.

"I knew you would find my back-tracks," he said slowly. "I was sure that you would come right back here."

"I knew where to look for you," Landon said quietly. "You've killed three lawmen, Farnol. The charge against you is murder!"

Farnol was breathing easily, and his lips parted in a slow taunting smile.

"I killed two of them, but you can't prove it," the gambler answered confidently. "I'm not through in Paradise yet, Landon. With you out of the way, folks will soon forget the little changes you made. Tiny Sutton does not amount to much, and I can round up a new gang for the asking!"

"I was afraid of that," Landon said softly. "I arrested you one time, Grant Farnol. I gave you another chance after *El Jornado de Muerte* had you whipped. I'm giving you still another chance."

"It took you long enough to come after me," the gambler

sneered. "For awhile I thought you'd got cold feet and had dogged it. I figured you had taken the easiest way and had run for the outside."

Landon shook his head slowly from side to side. He was watching the gambler, trying to read what was going on behind the hooded black eyes. Farnol showed little effects from his forced march across Hell's Basin, because of his tremendous vitality. Landon remembered the duty he had to perform.

"I kinda forgot about you for awhile, Farnol," Landon admitted honestly. "That was because Rory O'Hara hit me over the skull with his gun when I brought you up here for a change of clothes. You never did get the clothes. All I could remember was that I had beaten you, but I forgot that you had escaped."

"Out of your head, eh?" Farnol said nastily. "Things would have been some different had I known about your lapse of memory."

"I'm sure of it," Landon agreed. "But to bring the case up to date. I found your horse back there in the badlands where you made the change. That was after you had deserted your pard, Rory O'Hara."

"He stopped that damn sheriff's lead," the gambler answered callously. "I only nicked Sutton again, but the next time I'll get that runty son center."

Landon fought against the anger that flooded his veins like a raging torrent. The fingers of his right hand opened and closed spasmodically. Farnol watched with a knowing smile on his swarthy face.

"Do you want to gamble now?" he asked quietly.

"One way or the other, the result will be the same," Landon answered, his voice harsh and strained. "My orders were to bring you in—*dead or alive*. You've got a choice!"

"You'll have to take me dead, deputy," Farnol said lightly. "Where's the lost gold mine?"

Landon made no attempt to evade the direct question. He showed the confidence he had in his own ability when he answered Farnol with a glitter in his gray eyes.

"The mine is back in Eden Valley," he said. "There's an old river bed where the stream jumped her banks. I'll give the ranches back to the men of Paradise, Farnol. The ones you took away from them when they could not pay their taxes. Your money will go to the poor."

His voice lashed the gambler like a whip. Farnol smiled

and nodded his head. His left hand was hooked in his vest, with his right hovering above the holstered gun on his thick leg.

"It's your deal, lawman," he said quietly. "Call the turn!"

Landon sighed and shook his head slowly. "I'm remembering that I represent the law," he said wearily. "I've got to give you a chance to surrender. You'll get a fair trial by your betters."

"Take one step forward, and I'll come out smoking," Farnol warned. "I've waited for this chance to meet you, and I mean to settle a lot of old scores. I'm on one side; you're on the other. It lies between you and me as I see it. Make your fight!"

"You might change your mind," Landon said just above his breath. "I'll count up to three. Surrender by then, or I'm coming out on the last count."

There was no bravado in his quiet statement. His eyes were watching the gambler, studying the swarthy handsome face like a card player waiting, after making a heavy bet.

Farnol leaned forward and settled his weight. His black eyes stared at the deputy without winking. Landon spoke suddenly.

"One!"

Grant Farnol did not move. Landon moistened his lips and tolled off the second numeral.

"Two!"

He saw the gambler's eyes narrow down at the corners. Then Farnol jerked his vest and plunged his right hand under his left arm before the third count had been spoken.

Landon slapped down with the speed of long practice. His palm thudded against the walnut handle of his forty-five Colt. The long barrel snouted up over the lip of his holster just as metal flashed from the gambler's silk vest.

Landon felt the burn of the bullet against his ribs just as he slipped the hammer under his thumb. In that split second he *knew* that Farnol had beaten him to the draw. The two explosions were spaced so close that only a stuttering echo told the difference. They reverberated against the low ceiling like sullen thunder.

Farnol was swaying forward, trying to bring his hide-out gun up for a second shot. His face was twitching, and the veins stood out on his forehead with the effort he was making for a follow-up.

Landon bucked the smoking six-shooter down in his hand.

He held his second shot when he saw that Farnol would never make his raise. The gambler was calling on every bit of his will power to make his flagging muscles obey the commands of his brain. Now he was swaying slowly, with his black eyes half closed. He tried to move his feet for balance and failed. He crashed down to shake the room with his thudding bulk.

Joel Landon stepped back and waited until the echoes had died away. The smoke was still swirling through the room when a thunder of hooves rattled into the yard and slid to a stop near the front porch. A dozen men came through the door with cocked pistols in their hands. They stopped abruptly when they saw Grant Farnol down on the floor.

Scuffed boots rattled out a tattoo of defeat in the smoke-laden room. Landon reversed the gun in his hand and ejected the spent shell, automatically thumbing a fresh cartridge through the loading gate before sheathing the gun. His left hand went up to his vest and removed the shining badge of his office.

He faced a tall man who wore a gold badge on his faded vest. The stranger's hair was gray; he wore a small clipped mustache above stern, straight lips. Landon smiled wearily and held out his hand.

"There's your man, Marshal," he said slowly. "I gave him a chance to surrender and stand trial. He said he'd leave it up to old Judge Colt. I've finished my last job for the law, and I'm handing in my star!"

United States Marshal Bronson stepped back, shaking his head vigorously. He refused to take the badge.

"You can't do that, Joel," he argued sternly. "You've earned promotion for your work, and a heap of reward money. We heard what happened to Smiley, and I came up with the boys to help you finish the job you had started. You just can't quit the force!"

"You said to get Farnol, dead or alive," Landon answered patiently. "There he is. His horse is tied out at the back, and the saddle-bags are bulging with money. I've promised that money to the poor right here in Paradise. I'm turning in my badge, chief!"

U. S. Marshall Bronson knew that further argument was useless. He took the badge reluctantly and shook hands with a grip that told of his admiration. The men nodded silently when Landon walked through the kitchen and made his way to his horse. Now that the long search was ended, there was little more to be said.

Landon avoided the little town and followed a game trail into the shifting sands of Hell's Basin. A gentle breeze blew down from the north just as the last twilight faded. The stars began to cast a faint glow before they could be seen plainly. The desert seemed at peace, and Landon was a desert man.

While he rode through the night, Landon reviewed the events that had shaped his destiny since coming to the high desert. Adam Tyrone had insisted that he should be sent to Purgatory to do work that no one else could do. That work was now finished, and Joel Landon could think of himself. He could think about Eve Tyrone, and the promise he had made to her.

The moon was shining brightly when Landon rode across the last mile of Hell's Basin and sighted the green rocks that marked Dripping Springs. His horse was walking slowly when he passed the row of ghostly volcanic tombstones. Then they crossed the last sandy strip, and the thirsty horse stopped at the water-hole to drink.

Landon dismounted and faced the moist green rocks. He could see the new graves back in the deeper shadows. Joe Bodie's had been the first; the outlaws of Paradise now gave him ghostly company. The tall desert man sighed and pushed back his battered gray Stetson. This was rendezvous.

A tall figure came from behind the rocks and hesitated for a moment. The hesitation vanished when the girl ran out to meet him. Landon opened his arms and caught Eve Tyrone in a hungry embrace that had waited long, and had grown hungrier with waiting.

For a long time the only sounds came from the drinking horse down by the water-hole. The desert silence was soft and soothing. At last Eve whispered with her lips close to Landon's ear.

"I knew you'd come back, Joel. I never doubted it for a moment."

Joel Landon did not answer. He was slipping slowly to the ground, and the girl went with him to her knees to break his fall. She saw the dull splash of crimson on his gray wool shirt just below the heart. She ripped the heavy garment open with a little cry of fear bursting from her lips.

"You are wounded," she whispered. "Speak to me, Joel!"

"Just a scratch," Landon murmured drowsily. "Reckon I'm more sleepy than hurt."

Eve held him tightly when he sagged in her strong young arms. Then she laid him gently on the grass and filled his battered old hat with water from the spring. Five minutes later he opened his eyes slowly and tried to get to his feet. The girl tightened her arms and held him close to her breast.

"Just rest," she whispered, with her cheek against his hair. "I hear the men coming down to meet you."

"Help me to my feet," Landon pleaded. "I'd do the same for you, and I don't want them to see me down again!"

Eve Tyrone knew the depth of his pride, and she knew that he was thinking about their first meeting when the dreaded journey of death had taken his last ounce of strength. She helped him to his feet and supported him with her right arm. Landon spaced his boots carefully and caught his balance.

Adam Tyrone rode down through the pass with Tiny Sutton by his side. Doctor Telford was just behind, with the men of Purgatory riding in pairs. The old leader swung to the ground and came straight to Joel Landon. He gravely offered his right hand.

"Welcome home to Purgatory, son," he said clearly. "I notice that you do not wear your badge, so you must have finished your work."

Tiny Sutton advanced and offered his right hand. He drew Landon aside and whispered loud enough for all to hear.

"The boss of Paradise? Dead or alive, Joel?"

"Dead," Landon answered simply. "I forgot about that hide-out gun under his left arm, and I didn't have time to throw off my shot."

Tiny Sutton murmured his pleasure. For a moment he gripped Landon's hand, and then spoke with quiet content.

"I'm glad about that, Deputy. The folks back in Paradise won't have any more trouble, thanks to you, Joel. Neither will the folks here in Purgatory."

"I'm not a deputy any more, Tiny," Landon corrected quietly. "I promised Eve that I would turn in my star after I finished that one last job. Marshal Bronson rode up to Farnol's house, and I kept my promise."

"Might be just as well," Sutton said slowly. "You know all about minerals, and it will keep you busy developing that old Indian gold mine. What are you going to do with all that gold, Joel?"

"It belongs to Eve and old Adam," Landon said firmly.

126

"Half of it belongs to us," Tyrone corrected. "Eve told me something else after you left for Paradise."

Landon turned slowly and studied the old leader's smiling face. Then he glanced at Eve with a question in his eyes.

"I told Gramps," the girl said proudly, "that you would never leave us again."

"Did you tell him about you and me getting married one of these days soon?" Landon asked in a whisper.

"Tomorrow," the old leader spoke up quickly. "We are afraid that something might come up to make you change your mind, and I won't take any more chances. Am I right, Eve?"

"Right as rain, Gramps," the girl answered promptly. "And now you tell Joel the rest of it."

Landon swelled his deep chest and glanced from face to face. The riders of Purgatory were smiling broadly, waiting for old Adam to break the news. Tyrone stroked his long white beard and cleared his throat.

"I'm not asking you, Joel Landon," he began in a strong deep voice. "I'm telling you, and we will not take no for an answer. The men of Purgatory held a Council meeting, and they have elected you as their Mayor!"

"You can't do that," Landon objected. "You don't know me well enough, and I haven't been here long enough!"

"You will be here from now on," Tyrone answered with a broad smile. "And none of us would be here without your leadership. Congratulations, Mayor Landon. Now I can sit back and take my rest while you do all the work."

Doctor Telford came forward and offered his hand. His voice was vibrant with a new confidence when he offered his personal congratulations.

"I'm glad to see you again, Mayor Landon. And now, as your doctor, I want to look at the new wound you are trying to hide."

Landon shook hands and then drew away. Eve Tyrone was supporting him with her arm around his shoulders. Landon threw back his head and laughed happily.

"If I am the Mayor, I will give my first order, and I want it obeyed," he said with a chuckle. "You men ride on up the pass and leave me alone with my future wife."

"You are forgetting something, son," Adam Tyrone interrupted. "I would like to make a suggestion."

"We're listening," Landon agreed. "Speak out, Adam."

"You really found Eve back there in the Valley of Eden,"

Tyrone said with a broad smile. "Right where you found the old Indian mine. I thought it would be a good place to spend your honeymoon. We've fixed up the cabin some."

He mounted his horse and led his men up the pass while Eve and Landon tried to hide their embarrassment. Neither spoke until the hoofbeats had died away in the distance. Then Landon took the girl in his arms and kissed her tenderly.

"I have waited long to find you, Eve," he said slowly, but his throbbing voice told of his deep emotion. "I promise never to leave you again."

The girl's fingers touched the necklace of rough gold nuggets under his wool shirt. He removed it gently, placed it about her neck, and tucked it in place under her open collar. Her eyes closed when she gave him her lips, proudly, and without restraint. They looked out over the white sand in the yellow glow of the early sun. Peace had come to the desert, and to the riders of Purgatory.

ABERDEEN
CITY
LIBRARIES